THE FACELESS FUGITIVE

Six men went down into the old mine, but only three came up. As the last man out was hauled up, shots brought down the only surface shaft. The man, his face torn, held a revolver. He vanished on his way to hospital. Two days later, an unknown patient recovered consciousness in a nursing home, with no memory and his features swathed in bandages. When it became obvious that the police believed him a killer, he fought his way to the mine. But there, the mystery thickened.

ROBERT CHARLES

THE FACELESS FUGITIVE

Complete and Unabridged

LINFORD
Leicester

First published in Great Britain

First Linford Edition
published 1998

British Library CIP Data

Charles, Robert, *1938* –
    The faceless fugitive.—Laqrge print ed.—
Linford mystery library
    1. Detective and mystery stories
    2. Large type books
    I. Title
    823.9′14 [F]

    ISBN 0–7089–5337–9

Published by
F. A. Thorpe (Publishing) Ltd.
Anstey, Leicestershire
Set by Words & Graphics Ltd.
Anstey, Leicestershire
Printed and bound in Great Britain by
T. J. International Ltd., Padstow, Cornwall

This book is printed on acid-free paper

1

The Unknown Patient

He was alive. At least he thought he was alive. He came slowly from the depths of the unconscious. Struggling weakly, like a moth fighting clear of its cocoon, he emerged from darkness into darkness. And still he was unsure whether he was alive or dead.

He could see nothing and he could hear nothing. His body was held still by a soft but firm pressure all around him. He became aware of a dull ache in his limbs, a strange weakness as though the strength had been sapped from his muscles leaving them flabby and useless. He tried to stir, willing his legs to move. But the effort was too great. He had the feeling that he could have broken free from his weird, soft, prison, if only he were fit and strong.

If only he had the energy to move.

1

He summoned all his will power to the task of opening his eyes. The lids moved slightly, but something prevented them from opening, as though they were strapped down. He was afraid then: the fear seeping gradually through him like an alien ripple dancing through the red streams of his veins. His heart quickened with a staccato beat and he realized that he was breathing heavily. Sucking in air in sharp eager gulps as though each time he filled his lungs might be the last. The discovery that he was breathing steadied him and he began to relax. If he were breathing then he must be alive. It was a relief to be sure.

He relaxed for a long time; growing accustomed to his strange, close, surroundings; accepting the total enveloping darkness, and the lack of energy in his limbs. Slowly but surely he let his mind take over from his useless body.

His mind tackled the problem analytically, unhurriedly. He appreciated for the first time the fact that he was lying on his back, and he considered the closeness of his surroundings more carefully. His mind told him then that he was in a bed. He must be in a bed. In his present state that minor discovery became a great achievement.

The realization that he was in a bed, held only by a heavy covering of blankets, did a lot to ease his mind further. Before he had known nothing, but now that he knew that one thing he felt safe. Somehow it didn't seem feasible that any harm could come to him in a bed.

He made another attempt to move then, this time trying to lift his left arm. Pain stopped him. A sharp, knife-like pain that cut into his flesh just below his shoulder. So, his arm had been injured. Now he knew that much. His mind registered more pains then, dull aches that were not part of his general weakness. His right leg hurt, so did the lower regions of his back, his face felt very tender and smarted slightly. He wondered vaguely what had happened to him.

Tentatively he flexed the fingers of his right hand, feeling the smooth cotton of a sheet beneath the tips. There was no pain in that hand, no pain in the whole arm. At least his right arm was okay. He began to move it slowly, bringing his hand up over his waist to his chest. He found a loop of cord lying on his stomach and his exploring fingers traced it to the knot and the shape of a bow. It was a pyjama cord. He was wearing pyjamas. Another discovery. He was beginning to feel almost pleased.

He moved his hand carefully up his chest, running his finger tips along the edge of the pyjama jacket, climbing over the buttons. The weight of blankets on his wrist ceased suddenly and his hand was in the open. He touched his face cautiously. It was bandaged. A thick layer, that taped up his whole face, even his eyes. That explained the darkness, why he couldn't see or even raise his lids. His whole face and neck were thickly swathed in bandages. Only a minute little opening before his nostrils had been left to enable him to breathe.

He drew his hand back slowly. Now he knew something. He knew he had been hurt and someone had bandaged him and

4

put him to bed. He wondered how he had been hurt and who had taken care of him. He wondered where he was.

Then he began to wonder who he was. That last thought shocked him, chilling his body like a drenching of ice cold water. He didn't know his own identity. He didn't know his own name.

He tried to think of a name, hoping that the first one that came to mind might be his own. But the names he thought of were all jumbled together, and he knew that none of them were his. He tried thinking of other things then. Normal things like flowers and trees and streets. He found he could picture them quite clearly. He even conjured up a vision of Elizabeth Taylor in her latest film. The last was somehow reassuring. It was the kind of ordinary everyday thing that normal people would remember. People who had names and identities.

However he could remember nothing about himself.

He switched his mind on to a different track, searching all the possible explanations that might have brought him here. He had been in an accident, he was sure of that. Was it a car accident? Or perhaps a train crash or an aeroplane smash up? None of the suggestions stirred any reaction in his brain and he tried again. None of it helped and he gave up with a bitter feeling of failure.

For a while he lay in despair, hemmed in by silence and darkness, unknowing and unable even to think any more. Then the obvious occurred to him. Some person, or group of persons, had taken him in, bandaged his wounds and put him to bed. Eventually he, she, or they, had to return. Then he would be told what had happened. Who he was, and why he was here. All he had to do was wait. It was just a matter of waiting.

He would have smiled then if the swathed bandages had not held his face so firmly. Relief seemed to settle over him in a warm glow, soothing him with the knowledge that somewhere he had at least one friend. Somewhere there was someone who would be able to tell him all he needed to know.

Carefully he let his right hand wander

over his bandaged face, fingering the slightly fraying edges of cotton. When he pressed his face, it hurt and after that he made his fingers move gently. He toyed with the idea of pulling the wrappings away from his mouth and trying to attract some attention by shouting. But the slight pain when he pressed on the bandages warned him that he might do more harm than good, and it was only a matter of time anyway.

He listened carefully as he lay there, for the bandages had been applied to avoid covering his ears. He could hear nothing but the slight creak of the bed when he shifted his weight. The absolute silence began to prey on his nerves and he found himself remaining perfectly still in case he should miss some comforting natural sound. But there was no sound, and the fear he had experienced when he first recovered consciousness began to creep slowly back into his bones. Why didn't they come? Whoever had bandaged him and put him to bed — why didn't they come?

The time passed, but he had no idea

how quickly. The sensation of fear lingered with him and he had to fight down the urge to tear the wrappings from his eyes so that he could see. The silence seemed almost alive it was so complete. His left arm began to throb slightly and when he felt for it beneath his pyjama jacket he found it was bandaged from elbow to shoulder.

His strength had returned a little now and he decided abruptly that he was going to get up. If he couldn't shout then at least he would find something with which to make a noise. He was tired of lying still and waiting. Somehow he would make something happen.

He started to push himself up the bed, using his hips and his right elbow. His left arm hurt and he was afraid to trust it with any weight. As his right leg dragged up the bed he winced. There was another pain there; he seemed to be covered with minor pains and hurts beside his bandaged face and arm. It was as though he had collected a lot of cuts and bruises in a fall, but he couldn't remember falling from anywhere. He reached a

8

sitting position with less difficulty than he had expected. And then he had to lean a little to his left, he had collected some minor cuts in some inconvenient places as well.

He stayed like that for several minutes, contemplating his next move. Then he pushed back the bed clothes and cautiously swung his legs over the side. The floor was sharply cold to his feet and he thought instantly of linoleum. Linoleum was always cold. He straightened up slowly and found he could stand quite easily. Now that he had fully recovered there didn't seem to be a lot really wrong with him. At least nothing was broken. He wondered then how he was going to make enough noise to attract attention, and then another thought made him pause. For all he knew it might be night, and it would be hardly fair to arouse his host, or hosts, from their beds. He stood there undecided for a moment and then abruptly he heard the rattle of a door being opened.

He turned to face the sound and heard the faint swish as the door was pushed wide. A woman's voice — a startled woman's voice — said sharply, 'What are you doing? You shouldn't be out of bed.'

With his mouth bandaged he could make no answer, and he could only stand there feeling foolish and helpless as he listened to the sound of her shoes cross the room towards him. He heard the faint swish of her dress and then a hand, light and gentle, touched his shoulder.

'Come on, back into bed now.' Her tone had become low and sympathetic and he liked the sound of it. 'We didn't expect you to wake up so soon or you wouldn't have been left on your own.' She shepherded him back into bed and then her hand closed over his sound shoulder in a reassuring squeeze. 'Don't worry now. I'll go and fetch the doctor.'

He gave a slight nod of his head as she left him. There had been a brisk ring of authority in her tone and he decided that she must be a nurse. Evidently he was in a hospital. He spent the next few moments of waiting in wondering

10

whether the nurse would be blonde or brunette, and trying to decide what sort of features would best match the pleasant voice. He still hadn't made up his mind when the doctor entered his room.

He heard the sound of footsteps crossing to his bed, and then the man said: 'So you finally came round, young man. I'm sorry you had to wake up alone like that. I meant to have someone sitting with you, but I didn't expect you to recover so quickly. I'm really sorry. It couldn't have been a very pleasant awakening.'

He couldn't answer and the firm yet kindly voice went on. 'Now we're going to take these bandages off for you. Nurse, support the patient's head please.'

The patient felt gentle hands taking the weight of his head, and raised himself helpfully on to his elbows. He ignored the sudden pain as the bandage was stretched tight around his injured arm. More than anything else now he wanted those wrappings off his face so that he could see.

He felt them remove some safety pins

from above his left ear, and then the doctor began to unwind the bandages. He felt them pull as they travelled round his head, and winced.

'Easy now, easy,' murmured the soft voice of the nurse, and with an effort he relaxed.

The doctor added evenly, 'This may hurt a bit now, but don't try to say anything or jerk your head about. There are a lot of long cuts in your face and we've had to put several stitches in. We don't want them split open now, do we?'

The doctor's movements became slower as he neared the last of the bandages. He unwound them gently and the nameless patient felt them lifting from the skin of his temples. Something lifted above his right eye and the sharp pain told him that there was another cut there. He winced and stiffened and the hands that were removing the bandages became slower still. Carefully the doctor took the last strips from his eyes.

He hesitated before slowly opening his lids. The movement hurt above his right eye and he guessed that he had more stitches there. The seemingly large bulk of a lint or cotton pad overshadowed that one eye. He looked up at the doctor bending over him, a white haired man with fading blue eyes. He smiled and looked almost fatherly. To the doctor's right and just back out of his range of vision he heard the nurse but as yet he could not see her.

'Remember,' said the doctor carefully. 'Don't try to say anything when we uncover your mouth.' He went on gently unwinding the bandages, passing his hands deftly behind his patient's head.

When the last of them was removed he was finally allowed to lie back on the bed. There were more lint pads on his cheeks and the doctor removed them cautiously. His blue eyes were solemn for a moment, and then he smiled.

'The stitches are healing well. I think I can take them out shortly. Meanwhile I think you can talk if you try to do so without moving your jaw too much. Perhaps for a start you can tell me your name? Mine, by the way, is Howell.'

The question was like a slap in the face. The man with no identity stared dumbly, failing to grasp the meaning behind it. Failing because he wanted to. He had been so sure, relied so much on the hope that they would know. And now, abruptly, he was back where he had started when he first regained his senses, facing a blank past and an unforeseeable future.

He said hopelessly, 'You mean — ' A tight pain along his cheek brought back the doctor's warning and he started again through barely open lips. 'You mean you don't know?' His voice sounded cracked and squeaky, not how he expected his own voice to sound at all.

Uncertainty flickered in the doctor's gaze. 'No, young man, we do not. We only know that you were found near here. Lying in the road with your clothes in shreds, and your face torn and streaked with blood. When I examined you I found multiple cuts and grazes, plenty of bruises. I patched you up and had you put to bed. That's all I can tell you.'

The man with no name felt as if he

had received another slap across the face. He tried to make something out of the doctor's words but none of it made sense. He said at last. 'Didn't I have a wallet — anything with my name on?'

'No, no wallet.' His tone was regretful. 'The inside pocket of your jacket, where a wallet would normally be carried, had been ripped almost completely away.'

'What — what happened then? Was I in a car smash?'

'I don't think so. Your injuries were unlike any you might have received from being knocked down by a car. And no driver has reported any accidents along that road.'

He tried to think. 'Hit and run — could it have been hit and run?'

The doctor shook his head sadly. 'Like I said, you were suffering from the wrong kind of injuries for that kind of accident. Apart from those deep lacerations on your face I would have said you had had a fall, possibly down a steep hillside where you would have been buffeted about by bushes, rocks and so forth, as you fell. Does that help you?'

15

He moved his head vaguely in a tentative shake. 'No, I can't remember any fall. I can't remember anything.'

The nurse moved round into his range of vision, a dark haired girl with large brown eyes. The eyes were soft and pleasant like her voice and regarded him anxiously from beneath finely arched brows. 'Have you really tried to think now? Surely you must know something?'

He made a cautious shake of his head again. 'I was depending on you to tell me. I just — just don't know anything.'

Howell said slowly, 'You were found in the early hours of Monday morning, and it is now Tuesday afternoon. I kept you under for that time because you had obviously suffered some violent shock and needed the rest. The police have made efforts to trace your identity but have discovered nothing. I'm afraid you're a perfect mystery.'

The man on the bed felt a cold chill settle again in his stomach. The mention of the police stirred some sixth sense that made him suddenly afraid.

16

He didn't know why but he was afraid. Somehow he couldn't believe that he had committed any crime, but still the thought of the police filled him with fear. His mouth was very dry.

Howell didn't seem to notice his reaction. He went on, 'If it will help, you are in a private nursing home in Lincolnshire, some twenty miles from Lincoln. You were found practically on our doorstep.' He paused for an answer but when none came he said sadly, 'Well, I'd better replace those bandages. Don't worry, this time you'll be able to see.'

The nameless man suffered in silence as they re-bandaged his face. The new arrangement blotted out half his right eye but left the other one clear. A narrow slit was left for his mouth but he could only talk with difficulty. When it was done the dressings on his arm were changed. The whole area there was grazed and bruised as though he had fallen and slithered along a harsh surface or a grave road.

At last Howell stood up. 'Well, that's that. Now, how about a meal?'

For the first time he realized how hungry he was, and found time to wonder what and when he had last eaten. He said simply, 'I'm starving.' And found the words being strained through his almost closed mouth.

'Right then, Nurse Denning will see you fed. And I'll look in on you later tonight. Perhaps a little rest and time will help your memory to return.'

The man with no name watched him leave the room and then turned his attention to the nurse. Like all nurses she looked crisp and clean in her white uniform, the glossy black of her short hair spilled out in dancing curls from beneath her white cap. Her jaw line was a neat curve and her lips shaded a ripe cherry-pink. He decided it would be fun to kiss her, and laughed to himself at the thought that at least he hadn't forgotten all the important things.

She straightened his pillows and gave him a smile. 'Stay here now, and I'll be right back with your tea.'

She left the room briskly and he found himself watching the way the dark curls clustered at the nape of her neck. He thought it would be easy to fall in love with his nurse.

When she came back, she brought a tray containing tea and boiled eggs, plus a plate of buttered bread with the crusts neatly removed. A meal obviously chosen because it would not require much chewing and would not therefore disturb his stitches. He learned while he ate that there were several deep lacerations down his face, the worst being the sewn up gash in his cheek. Another shorter cut above his eye had also had to be stitched, but the remaining scratches across his features needed only bandaging. The closest she could get to describing them was by saying that it looked as though something had clawed at his face. Possibly a cat or some large wild bird.

He finished his meal and she took the tray away.

'You eat well anyway,' she said. 'Whatever happened to you I think it must have left you a lot more shocked and exhausted than physically hurt. Once your face and arm clears up you'll be pretty fit.' On that cheerful note she left him and went out.

For almost an hour he pursued the baffling mental problems surrounding his past. But he got nowhere. Then abruptly he heard a sound in the passage outside his room again, and then the rattle of the knob as the door was opened.

He looked up as Doctor Howell came in. The man's blue eyes were angry and his mouth set tight. Behind him were two tall men both wearing raincoats. The way Howell looked back to glower at them said as plainly as words that they were the reason for his suppressed anger.

The man with no name guessed who they were before the doctor spoke. And the realization sent the familiar cold chill through him again. His mouth was suddenly dry and he had to pass his tongue quickly across his lips.

Howell said tightly, 'I'm sorry, sir, but these men insist on seeing you tonight — they're policemen.'

2

A Stranger Calls

The unknown patient made an effort to still his vague fears as the doctor introduced the two police officers. The taller of the two was identified as Detective-Inspector James. The leaner, wiry man beside him was Detective-Sergeant Willet. Howell stopped at the foot of the bed and waited. It was clear that he meant to stay through the interview.

The two detectives pulled a couple of chairs up to the bed and sat down. 'How are you feeling, sir?' asked James pleasantly.

'Not too bad.' He was cautious.

'Then you won't mind if we ask a few questions. There's nothing to worry about of course. We'd just like to know who you are and how you came to be lying in the road nearby.' The man's voice had a softening Scottish burr to it and for a policeman he had a very frank smile.

'Then I'm afraid I can't help you. I was hoping that they were things that you could tell me.' The man with no name spoke calmly, but inside he was still uneasy.

'Yes, so Doctor Howell has been telling us. He seems to think that whatever kind of an accident you were involved in must have been coupled with a very great shock. Something pretty ugly that you want to forget. That's why your memory has gone blank on you. Deep down inside you don't want to remember at all.' He paused a moment then added: 'But unfortunately we have to know.'

The sergeant put in quietly, 'Haven't you any idea how you received your injuries, sir?'

'Haven't you?' He had the feeling that he shouldn't have asked and that the less he said and the sooner they left him the better. But he had to know. He went on. 'You must have made inquiries.'

James nodded. 'Sure we made inquiries, but they led us nowhere. You see we had nothing to go on. The way your face has been slashed it was difficult to get an accurate photograph. We circulated a likeness drawn by a police artist and most of the big papers printed it. But it was far from perfect and so far no one has recognized it.'

The vague fear seemed to harden in his stomach. He had only been unconscious for thirty hours, yet already the police had gone to the extent of printing his picture in all the daily papers. Why? Where was the need for all their haste? They couldn't possibly have known that when he did come round his memory would be a blank. So why all the hurry to trace his identity?

James was watching him closely. He said quietly, 'Will you try and think now, sir? Could it possibly have been a car accident you were in?'

'I don't know, I can't be certain, but I don't think so.'

'Do you think it was a fall you had? That seems to be the doctor's opinion.'

'Again I don't know.'

'Did you get in a fight or anything?'

'I don't know.'

'Did you get caught in a roof fall of any kind?'

He tensed and his whole nervous system tingled to a sudden note of warning. James was watching him closely. Too closely. The soft Scottish burr hadn't changed when that last question was put, but he was suddenly certain that that was the one all the others had been leading up to. But why should James think he had been trapped under a falling roof? And what kind of roof? He wanted to ask, to find out what the other man was holding back. But he didn't. He said flatly. 'I don't know.'

James smiled and took up the questioning again. Making more suggestions, trying to coax him into accepting one of the offered explanations. For over twenty minutes he talked before asking suddenly.

'By the way, sir, what newspaper did you work for?'

He was startled. Almost startled into giving an answer. For a second a reply seemed to hover in the back of his mind hesitating uncertainly before fading back into darkness.

'I — I don't know if I did work for a newspaper.' He faltered at last.

From the foot of the bed Howell said curtly: 'I told you his loss of memory was genuine. There's no point in firing trick questions.'

'Just a shot in the dark, Doctor.' James defended himself easily. 'It does no harm and often gives a lot of help.'

The man on the bed remained silent, his sense of caution preventing him from pursuing the matter. He knew instinctively that they would tell him nothing anyway. What they knew they were keeping to themselves, hoping to trap him into an admission of some kind. So he kept his thoughts to himself, telling them nothing until they finally tired and left him with a solemn promise to return.

An hour later the nurse brought him some supper on a tray. As he ate she said quietly, 'Did those policemen help you to find out who you are?'

He looked at her warily through his one eye. 'No, but they did give the impression that they knew more than I did.'

She smiled. 'Don't worry about it. Some of your friends or relations will turn up to claim you in time.'

'I sincerely hope so, otherwise I look like being a nameless nobody for the rest of my life.'

'You won't. Your memory will return in time. And until then you can choose any name you like. What would you like to be called?'

He stopped eating. 'I don't know, I hadn't thought about it.'

'Well, think. We must start calling you something mustn't we?'

He smiled cautiously behind his mask of bandages. 'Why don't you choose? You can have the honour of christening me.'

The cherry lips pursed thoughtfully. 'Something nice and easy I think. How about Larry? I once had a boy-friend called Larry.'

He laughed softly. 'If it was good enough for a boyfriend of yours it's good enough for me. You never know, I might take on more of his good fortunes than just his name.'

Her eyebrows lifted primly but the brown eyes beneath were smiling. 'Whoa now! It's unconventional to try and get fresh with your nurse these days. Besides, the original Larry got his face slapped and my big brother almost threw him out of the door.'

'Then perhaps we'd better think of another name — quickly.'

'Oh, no, I'm beginning to think it suits you. And you gave me the privilege of selecting it — remember.'

'Okay. Larry I'm named, and Larry I'll stay. Now what do I call you?'

'Nurse, or if you want the full title, Nurse Denning.'

He finished the last sandwich and protested heartily. 'Unfair, and we were getting on so well.'

She laughed. 'Sorry, Larry, but that's the way it is. Now finish up that tray so that I can take it with me. I'm not supposed to devote too much time to any one patient.'

'Okay.' He deliberately lingered over

the last of his meal while she talked. When it was finished he submitted to being tucked up again and found himself wishing she would kiss him good night. It was a pleasant dream but an unrealized one.

As she left, she called out cheerfully, 'Good night, Larry.'

'Good night.' Larry, as he was already beginning to think of himself, watched the door close behind her regretfully. He had taken an instant liking to Nurse Denning. There was something in her smile that stirred him inside. He lay back and with unexpected ease fell asleep.

* * *

Early the following afternoon he had another visitor, this time an unexpected one. He came in with Howell, a tall, gaunt, man with clear green eyes. He wore a brown flecked sports jacket with a plain yellow tie. When he took his hat away he revealed a thick layer of sandy-coloured hair.

Howell said cheerfully, 'I've got a

visitor for you, young man. Mr. Rogart. He believes you might be a missing friend of his.'

The gaunt man came over to the bed and looked down, studying the patient carefully. 'Do you know me, son?' he asked.

Larry — he had fully accepted the name in place of his own — eyed him uneasily. He couldn't remember ever seeing the man before and slowly shook his head.

'Well?' Howell's voice was eager.

Rogart looked up. 'He doesn't seem to know me, Doctor, and with his face covered up like that I can't really tell.' He had a slight Scottish accent and Larry was reminded of the soft-spoken Inspector James. This man talked in much the same way. Rogart went on. 'Perhaps if I could talk to him a while?'

Howell suddenly looked doubtful, as though he were not quite sure whether that would be the right thing.

Rogart went on, 'If I were to talk to him, about things and people he should know, I might jog his memory.'

'And if he isn't the man you believe he is?'

'If he isn't, then I'll have wasted my time. But there'll be no harm done. And I shall have to talk awhile before I can be sure. Those bandages around his face don't even let him speak very clearly. From just looking at him I can't really tell.'

'All right then.' Howell sounded reluctant. 'But I shall have to leave you with him. I'm afraid I have other patients to attend to. I'll give you fifteen minutes.'

'Thank you, Doctor. That should be sufficient, one way or another.'

Howell hesitated, a doubtful expression still on his kindly face. Then abruptly he went out and closed the door behind him.

Rogart remained standing, a slight smile playing around the corners of his lean mouth. The clear green eyes looked very sharp and almost frightening.

Larry found his voice and said slowly, 'Well, Mr. Rogart, who do you think I am?'

'I have no idea.' Rogart sat on the

30

edge of the bed facing him. 'Not that it matters. I have no doubt that you know perfectly well who you are.'

The flat simplicity of the statement left Larry momentarily stunned. The green eyes regarded him with a flicker of amusement and a tight knot of anger coiled inside him. He drew himself up on one elbow and then the same sense of caution that had prevented him from talking to the police held him back. He said tightly. 'What's that supposed to mean?'

Rogart chuckled softly. 'I mean you may have successfully fooled the police but you cannot fool me. You see, I happen to know why it is so convenient for you to lose your memory. The police do not.'

For a moment he thought of pressing the bell-push above his bed and having Howell throw his unwanted visitor out. But again there were new questions with answers he had to know. Forcing himself to relax he said warily. 'What makes you think I'm faking a loss of memory? Who are you anyway?'

'Call me an interested party. I may not know who you are, in fact I don't even care. But I do know part of what happened to you and I want to know the rest. In fact I'm in the same position as the police. Only I can guess at what you might have found down there. That's how I know this loss of memory tale is a fake.'

'You're wrong, mister. I haven't a clue as to what you're talking about.'

Rogart laughed. 'All right, let's stop playing. Alone, and in your present condition you haven't a hope in hell of making any profit out of your discovery. So I propose we do a deal — form a partnership so to speak. You tell me exactly what happened down there and then leave the rest to me.'

'Down where?'

'Down the old McArnot mine of course. Where else?'

The name meant nothing to Larry. He lay back watching Rogart's face and feeling slightly bewildered. 'Supposing you tell me what and where this place is?'

The man's lean mouth tightened and he looked angry. 'The McArnot mine is an old coal-mine on the north-west coast of Scotland. It's in Sutherland near Shieldonnel cove. Now supposing you tell me what happened in the old workings of that mine?'

'And how should I know?'

'Because you were there. You were the last man to come out of those old workings alive. I want to know what happened down there, what you found, and what you did to the three men with you. It's my belief you murdered them.'

'Murder.' The echoes of the word seemed to wash over him in an icy chill and then settle in a freezing block in the pit of his stomach. 'What do you mean — murder?'

'What else could it be? You had a gun in your hand when they pulled you up, and there were three shots missing from it. One for each man in the mine.'

'You're crazy.' The words slipped jerkily through his lips. 'You must be crazy.'

'Am I?' Rogart's smile was back again.

'Why don't you pack it up? If the police don't get it out of you I will, and I'd rather be first.'

'I just don't know what you're talking about.'

'All right then, we'll go through it slowly. I'll tell you all I know and you fill in the blanks. On Sunday morning there was a roof fall in the west gallery of the new workings. It blocked up almost a hundred yards of the tunnel and bottled up a whole load of equipment at the pit face. Fortunately, being a Sunday, there were no miners at the face. However the equipment that was bottled up there was worth quite a packet. They were using some new type drills and so forth, and then there was the coal seam still to be mined. The owners started to make plans for clearing the tunnel and then found when they inspected it that the roof was still liable to collapse. It was too dangerous to work beneath it, so they hit on another idea. One of the galleries of the old workings runs parallel to and a little below the west gallery. They figured if the old workings were safe enough to work in they could break through from there. So, they sent a party of five men down to inspect that old gallery — and that's where you came in.'

Larry swallowed a mouthful of air, feeling his larynx rise as he worked his throat. 'How do I come in?' he demanded.

'You approached Lucas, the assistant mine manager who was leading the party, asking him if you could go along.'

'Why should I want to go along?'

Rogart smiled. 'I don't doubt that the story you told was true. I don't see how you could possibly have known what was down that mine until you stumbled across it. With Konrad dead I'm the only man alive who knows it's there.'

'Who the hell is Konrad — and how did he die?'

'You wouldn't know him, and he died of quite natural causes. Natural in those times anyway.'

'All right then.' Larry was keeping a tight rein on his temper. Refusing to be aroused by the man's infuriating manner.

'What is this story I'm supposed to have told this man Lucas?'

'That you were a journalist. A freelance writer of some kind. You'd written an article around the fishing boats that sailed from Shieldonnel and now you felt you were on the track of another story.'

With a surge of alarm Larry remembered the disarming smile of Inspector James. And the man's subtle shot in the dark. James too had believed him to be a journalist.

Rogart went on easily. 'You showed Lucas a membership card from some writing association or other. On the strength of that he took you below. I believe the police are doing a mass check on all writing associations and such like now. They hope to find one with someone fitting your description among the membership lists. However they've got a bit of a job on. The only man who knew which organization issued that membership card was Lucas, and he's still in the mine. Probably dead. No one else got a good look at the card. There was no reason for them to bother. You gave your name of course but that isn't helping them much. There's a hell of a lot of Browns in the British Isles.'

Larry said quietly, 'And you think I'm this mystery journalist named Brown. What makes you so sure? And what happened at that mine?'

'Still playing innocent. Haven't I convinced you yet?' He chuckled again, a glint of humour showing in the green depths of his eyes. 'All right, so we'll go on with the story-telling. You went below with Lucas and those other four men. You went down the main shaft into the old workings, the only shaft that's still open. The wooden ladders on the sides were so rotten you had to descend with the help of ropes. You were gone almost an hour, checking the state of the props in the tunnels and the shoring on the walls.' He paused. 'Don't you remember it, Mr. Brown?'

'It means nothing to me,' Larry was surprised at the cracked sound his voice had suddenly acquired. But he was speaking the truth. Rogart's tale had stirred nothing in his memory.

The gaunt man looked angry again. 'You know, you're trying my patience Mr. Brown. But to continue: You returned to the foot of the shaft with the others when the survey was completed. And the first two men went up the rope. Then something happened, something that only you can tell about. Those first two men came up in perfectly good health, and reported that everything was just as it should be below. The other four men were patiently waiting for their turn to be hauled up the, shaft.'

He stopped again as if waiting for Larry to say something, but when the other remained silent he went on. 'They started to haul you up the shaft and then it happened. There was a scream from below, shouts and the sound of a scuffle. And then there came three distinct reports from a revolver. The roar of the explosions in that narrow space brought the rotten walls of that old shaft crashing down. The men above hauled you up to the top and had you nearly out when the rest of the shaft caved in. Once the bottom had collapsed there was nothing to stop the upper sides falling in as well. You were quite understandably crazy from fear and shock when they lifted you out. The sensation of being buried alive in that falling shaft must have been enough to send anyone's mind temporarily blank.'

He paused again for effect and then finished. 'Your face was a bloody mess from a lot of deep slashes that you couldn't possibly have got from the falling rocks and dirt. How you got those I don't know. But in your hand you held a gun. The gun that had brought the shaft down — and fired the three shots that must have killed those other three men.'

3

Night Visitor

Larry realized suddenly that he was sweating, and yet he was cold. Rogart's story of the McArnot mine meant nothing to him, but it fitted. The multiple scratches and bruises that covered his body could be explained if he had been caught in a falling mine shaft. And the horror of it could have been subsconsciously responsible for cutting all memory of it from his mind. He thought of James then. If Rogart's story of the mine disaster were true then the policeman also obviously suspected him of being the mysterious journalist. James's questions all pointed to that; his reference to a newspaper and the suggestion that he, Larry, might have been trapped in a roof fall.

Larry looked up and then found himself unable to break his gaze away from

Rogart's clear green eyes. The gaunt man was smiling faintly, his lean capable fingers drumming slowly and lightly on the bed. He was very sure of himself, very very sure. Inspector James must have been pretty sure as well. And Larry? Larry wasn't sure at all.

Rogart said easily, 'The police are as certain as I am that you were the last man out of that mine. Only they're stalled for a bit by this loss of memory tale. That fool doctor out there is completely taken in and they're accepting his word for it. But it won't last. Eventually they're going to get tough and tell Howell to keep his nose out of it. You'll need a friend then, and that's where I come in. I might be able to get you out of the country, providing you help me first.'

Larry needed time to think. Plenty of time to think. As much to make time as to get an answer he asked, 'Supposing I am this man you're looking for. How am I supposed to have got down here to Lincolnshire?'

'Cadging lifts I suppose, or stowing

away aboard lorries travelling the Great North Road. We're not very far from that. When you were taken out of the mine you were in too bad a state to do any talking so you were bundled into a hastily called ambulance and sent to the nearest hospital, which was a fair distance away. When the ambulance got there you had vanished and the back door was swinging. Apparently you must have jumped for it when they slowed down for a hill or a bend. I suppose your next thought then was to get away as far south as possible. Your luck must have been running high for somehow you got right down here before you finally collapsed from exhaustion.'

'That's *if* I'm the man you think I am.'

'Don't be daft man, with your kind of injuries who else could you be? You're not going to tell me that one badly hurt man with his face slashed to ribbons could vanish from one spot and an identical man without a memory turn up in another without there being a connection. How you got here I don't know, but I do know you're the same man.'

Larry decided abruptly that it was time he got rid of his unwelcome visitor. He wanted to be alone in order to think. To sort out the possibilities of this fantastic tale on his own. He said flatly, 'I think you've got the wrong man Mr. Rogart. Whatever happened to me I'm sure I haven't murdered anybody down any old mine shafts. I think you'd better go.'

Rogart's eyes narrowed. 'Mr. Brown, I came here to find out what happened down the old McArnot mine. And I'm going to find out. You were the last man to come out of that shaft alive — and you're going to tell me.'

Larry said suddenly, 'Who are you anyway? Why is it so important to you what happened down there?'

'I didn't come here to answer questions, only to ask them. Never you mind what it means to me.'

'Okay, it doesn't really matter because I know nothing about it anyway.'

The twist of Rogart's mouth made him look suddenly vicious. 'So that's the way you want to play it is it. Well just take a wee spot of advice, Mr. Brown. When I leave here I'm going to tell that doctor that I was wrong about you. That you're not the missing friend I thought you might be. If you're wise you'll play up to that and let him think that I talked only of people and places I thought you'd know. You'll find it's better for both of us that way.'

Larry watched him grimly. 'And supposing I don't. Supposing I tell him the truth?'

'Then it's your funeral. There's nothing the police or anyone can charge me with at the moment. But if the police should discover that you know all I've told you then they'll get a lot tougher with you. At the moment your doctor is fighting tooth and nail to hold them off, claiming that you stand a much better chance of regaining your memory under his methods than theirs. So you see, the longer you can keep up this pretence to the police the better it will be for you. Eventually you may have to face a treble murder charge, and it'll do you no particular good to bring it on any sooner than you have too.'

'But I'm pretty sure I'm not the man they're looking for.'

'Only pretty sure? Why not wait until you're absolutely certain before you tell them.' He stood up slowly from the edge of the bed. 'I'll give you time to think it over, Brown, and I'll come back again. I shall have to use another method of entry of course, I won't be able to bluff my way in a second time. But I'll find a way. Maybe by then you'll have come to your senses and we can join forces to solve both our problems. You can tell me what happened down the mine, and I'll see if I can save you from hanging.'

Larry said angrily, 'I was never in the mine.' The sharp way he said it made his cheek hurt and he had to bite his lip. For a horrible moment he thought he had wrenched some of the stitches out.

Rogart smiled grimly. 'Think it over. You were the last man out of that mine. And unless you want to dangle at the end of a rope, you'd better play along with me.'

He picked up his hat and pushed his sandy hair beneath it as he settled it on his head. He smiled again, and calmly left.

Larry watched him go, his heart hammering and his mouth dry. For a while his mind seemed too numb to think clearly but at last he forced himself to review the few facts he now knew.

For a start Rogart's story if it were true would fully explain his present condition. Secondly, some of the questions phrased by Inspector James seemed to indicate that there might be something to it. He recalled abruptly that James too had been a Scot. His voice betrayed that. It was possible that James was not a Lincolnshire C.I.D. officer, but had been sent down specially from Scotland. His thoughts became tangled again and he had to stop. His head was beginning to ache.

He tried to make his mind go blank for a few moments in order to rest, but the memory of the gaunt stranger and his story of the old mine stuck in his brain. Finally he made another attempt to face the problem rationally. If only he knew whether an incident such as Rogart had described had taken place it would have helped. But without asking Howell or the nurse he had no way of knowing and to have asked them would have drawn a lot of unwanted questions he was not yet ready to face.

For a moment he decided to assume that Rogart's story must be true. What reason could the man have to make up such a tale? That raised the question of why hadn't the story jogged his sleeping memory? And the only answer seemed that whatever had happened to him in the bowels of the earth had been too horrible for his memory to retain it. The whole affair was strangely mixed up, like a third rate film that could be plausible if only the director had knotted the dangling ends. Only in this case he had to trace the threads and tie them himself, or else they might finish up by weaving themselves into a noose for his neck.

A new thought struck him then. If the police were waiting for his memory to return in order to question him properly, it was unlikely that Rogart would have been allowed to see him first. The thought heartened him a little until he realized that Howell might have defied the police demands if he thought it would benefit his patient. Howell was that kind of doctor. Larry knew then that he was right back where he had started. Whichever way he looked at things it was always the same. He just didn't know anything.

He finally gave it up and waited for Howell and Nurse Denning to come and change his bandages. He had vague hopes that one of them might volunteer some more information without his asking, but when they came their talk told him nothing new. He guessed that Rogart had departed without arousing the suspicions of either of them, but his own uncertainty restrained him from asking any questions about the man.

★ ★ ★

Larry awoke late that night. He opened his one unbandaged eye and stared up

48

at the ceiling, feeling vaguely uneasy in the darkness. Nurse Denning had drawn the curtains earlier in the evening so that now the room was pitch black. He lay there motionless with his ears alert, listening to the silence. He could feel the regular thump of his own heart but he was conscious of nothing else. Yet he couldn't relax. Something had tightened the muscles of his body and tensed his nerves. He wondered what had awakened him.

There was no explanation. Nothing. But the vague uneasiness persisted. He hadn't woken up normally. Something had jerked him out of his sleep. Normally he would have wakened slowly, blinking and unwilling to stir. Tonight something had snapped him wide awake, instantly alert.

He kept on listening. He could see nothing but he had the feeling that it was his ears that had brought him that vague warning. The air in his room seemed very still and his chest began to hurt. He realized abruptly that he was holding his breath, and he let it out slowly and soundlessly. It was then that he heard a sound.

It was an alien sound, a kind of sharp scratching noise as though someone had lightly scraped two pieces of broken glass together. It came from the french windows behind the long curtains.

Larry waited, still listening. It came again, coupled with a slight muffled rustle that barely reached him through the gloom. He was certain that someone was standing outside the windows, trying to force a way in.

He thought instantly of Rogart. The tall gaunt man had promised him that he would return, even though he had to find some other method of entry. Could this be what he meant, breaking in at the dead of night?

The sounds came again and Larry felt his heart beat just a little faster. He lay still and silent in his bed, all his senses wary and alert, trying to build a more complete picture of what was happening from the slight noises that reached his ears. He felt the hair prickle on the back of his neck and he moved his tongue nervously in his dry mouth. He wondered how many men there were outside and realized with a little shudder of fear that he was very vulnerable lying flat on his back. He wouldn't be able to put up any kind of a fight in his bed, held down by the weight of the blankets.

Very cautiously he attempted to pull the coverings aside but they had been well tucked under the bed. For the first time he wished that Nurse Denning wasn't quite so neat and efficient. He raised himself slightly and then froze as the bed uttered a gentle creak. He remained there listening, but the soft menacing sounds at his window went on without pause. Carefully he pulled again at the blankets and felt them pull out from under the mattress. He pushed them back towards the foot of the bed and felt abruptly cold as he exposed his body to the night air.

He stayed there for a moment, supported by his elbows and trying to decide on his next move. Then he swung his legs silently over the edge of the bed, towards the french windows. The bed creaked again as he straightened up and again he froze into a silent, listening, statue.

The sounds outside stopped and the very air seemed to thicken with the tension as he waited for them to start again.

After a few moments they did and he expelled his breath slowly. A small bedside table with an antique vase of flowers was near his right hand and he picked it up carefully. He removed the flowers and laid them back on the table, the vase he held low with his fingers coiled round the long stem-like neck. Moving silently towards the window, his bare feet muffled by the carpet, he saw that the curtains had been left an inch or two apart. From this new angle he could see through the gap but at first he could make nothing out. Then he recognized the outline of the door frame and the outline of a shadow behind the glass. It was a tall shadow, topped by the shape of a trilby hat. The outline fitted the mysterious Mr. Rogart well, but Larry couldn't be sure that it was him.

There was a sudden gentle click

from behind the curtains and then the slight sounds ceased. Larry waited, dry mouthed, and with his stomach fluttering vaguely. The ugly grazes on his left arm began to irritate and he felt an almost overpowering urge to start scratching at the bandages. The cold neck of the vase was clamped tightly in his fingers, held more securely by fear than if it had been grafted into his hand.

Then abruptly there was an almost inaudible squeak and one half of the french windows began to move tentatively inwards. Larry watched through the thin gap in the curtains, knowing he was hidden in the darkness of the room. He saw the door edge open until the fingers of a hand slid through the gap. The fingers tightened on the door edge and slowly eased it open. Behind the glass he could make out the white blur of a face below the trilby hat.

Grimly Larry raised the vase for a blow, bringing it up sharply and silently above his head. And in that instant a miniature flood of ice-cold water gushed out of the open mouth of the vase and shot down his uplifted arm. The sudden shock drew a startled gasp of alarm from his lips and the unknown intruder whirled abruptly away from the half open windows.

Larry swore and dropped the vase with a sudden crash on the floor. He shook his arm violently and then plunged through the curtains to wrench the door fully open. The intruder was already diving into the shubbery across the narrow lawn and he ran after him with a sudden determination to catch him. Now that his midnight visitor was running from him he had no more fear of the man. Only a fierce desire to come to grips with him and beat some answers out of him. There were so many questions that he felt the man could answer.

The close-cropped grass was damp and cold to his feet but he ignored it, crashing into the shrubbery in the wake of his fleeing visitor. Leafy branches whipped at him as he forced his way through, but he kept on following the sound of the man ahead. There was soft earth here and the soil clung to his bare soles as he raced over it, and then abruptly the crashing sounds of the man ahead stopped.

Larry halted, braking clumsily by catching at a passing shrub. He held on to it with one hand as he gulped down the chill night air and listened for the movements of his quarry. A scuffing sound drew him into pursuit again and he raced out on to the gravel path. On the opposite side the fleeing intruder was then vanishing into a small wooded copse.

More footsteps caught his attention then and he glanced round to see another figure sprinting towards him down the drive that obviously led back to the house. Larry hesitated and then dashed after his quarry. The man had completely disappeared among the young trees. Larry reached the first of them, sprawling young birches with silvery trunks, and then abruptly his foot caught in a root and he blundered heavily forwards.

He was up almost instantly but that brief fall had been enough. A hand closed on his shoulder and dragged him to a stop. He lunged away jerkily but another hand fastened on his wrist and he couldn't break the hold.

'Stop it,' a voice said angrily. 'Stop acting like a fool.' It was Nurse Denning.

4

Breakout

Larry turned to stare into the thickening shadows that merged into total blackness among the closely grouped clusters of birch. There was no longer any sign of the unknown intruder who had tried to break into his room. There was no sound either. Whoever the man was, he had got clean away.

The nurse asked breathlessly, 'What's the matter with you? Why were you running away?'

Larry faced her. She was muffled in a wide-collared grey coat, the wavy delicate curls of her dark hair falling even farther forward around her temples without the restraining white cap. Her eyes and the cherry lips were set angrily.

He said slowly, 'Didn't you see him?'

'See him? See who?'

Stupid question, he thought to himself.

The man had already been in the shadow of the woods when he came out on to the drive. Obviously the girl hadn't seen him. Aloud he said, 'I was chasing a man. He tried to break into my room and I followed him this far before he vanished in these woods.'

Her eyes took on a stern, disbelieving look. She smiled faintly. Her face was flecked by slightly moving shadows cast by the leafy branches of birch. It was like a stranger's face, different to how she looked in the bright light of his room.

'Are you sure?' she asked, and her voice sounded brisk and impersonal, like a nurse's voice again.

'I'm sure,' he told her. 'I don't know who he was or what he wanted. But he was there. And I chased him this far before I lost him.' He relaxed a little as he spoke, knowing that there was nothing he could do about finding his quarry now.

She felt the stiffness go out of him and slackened her grip on his arm. 'Why should anyone want to break in after you?'

58

'How should I know? I don't even know who I am.'

'Of course, I'm sorry, Larry. Here, you're shivering.' She let go of his arm and started to wriggle out of her heavy coat. 'Put this on, and let's get back inside.'

He suddenly realized that he was wearing only pyjamas. Until she had mentioned it he hadn't noticed how cold he really was. Now he began to shiver and made no objection when she helped him into her grey coat.

She looked down at his feet and made a little tongue clicking noise of despair.

'No shoes either! Haven't you any sense? You'll catch your death of cold running about bare-footed.' She lifted his chin suddenly and studied his bandaged face. 'Well, at least you don't seem to have done any damage there. You might have busted those stitches open.'

Her attitude irritated him and he had to quell an angry retort. What she was thinking he couldn't tell, but he was sure that she didn't believe his story. Maybe she thought he had been running away.

Or sleepwalking in a nightmare. She took his hand firmly and pulled him towards the gravel path. 'Come on, it's bed for you.'

Larry allowed himself to be led up the path towards the house. It was almost a mansion, low-roofed but covering a wide area. A couple of tall poplars grew up against one wall and nearly all of the many windows were in darkness. Like a hospital there would be a certain time for lights out. There was an iron-railed balcony running along the level of the second floor and below that parts of the walls, mostly of old flint, were clothed in ivy. The square blocks of the chimney stacks made clumsy silhouettes against the skyline of the roof.

Larry turned his attention to the grounds, feeling vaguely that later it might prove an asset to know something of the layout of the place. On his left was the shrubbery and on his right the birch copse thinned out and gave way to another lawn, studded with evergreens and odd fruit trees, that appeared to run up past the house. He had no doubt that somewhere behind him at the other end of the drive there would be a road, possibly the road where he had been found unconscious.

The drive ended before a pillared porch that led on to the main entrance. But before they reached it the nurse turned off the gravel and led him across the lawn to his room. As he pushed through the curtains a piece of the broken vase crunched under her foot and she stopped with a start.

He said lamely, 'I'm sorry. I broke the flower vase.'

She said sharply, 'Wait here then, or you'll cut your feet.'

She left him and crossed the room to flick on the light. As she turned back he picked his way into the room and almost quailed under the glint in her eyes. She glared down at the shattered vase in its pool of spilt water.

'All right,' she said. 'I don't suppose you did it out of malice. What was the reason?'

He drew a deep breath, met her eyes, and told her.

When he finished she was frowning. She said slowly, 'Who would want to break in here? And why?' There was a strong note of doubt in her tone.

He hesitated for a moment, then offered quietly, 'Rogart had a reason.'

The answer caught her unawares and uncertainty flickered in her brown eyes. 'What sort of reason?'

He looked away and hesitated much longer this time. But somehow he trusted her. Besides it was suddenly clear that he had to trust someone. Alone he was waging a hopeless battle, for he knew nothing of the odds that faced him. Eventually he would have to tell someone. He looked back and slowly told her all about Rogart.

She listened without interrupting. Her eyes never once left his face and he had the feeling that she was seeing right through him, bandages and all. However, when he stopped talking the neat line of her jaw was set hard, and the serious lines of her face told him that this time she believed him.

She said quietly, 'And you think that

Rogart tried to break in here tonight, just to find out if you had decided to help him.'

'I suppose so. But I can't help him. I don't know anything.' He shrugged his shoulders helplessly.

'Hmmm,' she looked up and gave him a sudden smile. 'You know what I think? I think you're worrying too much. Rogart must be a crank.'

Her bland answer brought a trapped feeling around him again and he found he couldn't think of anything else to say. Still smiling she went on. 'Now just you forget him and get back into bed.'

He suffered in silence as she fussed around him. She stripped off his wet things and dried him with a towel before tucking him back into bed. He was both grateful and resentful. He wasn't quite sure how he could experience the two different emotions at the same time, but he did.

At last she made an attempt to draw back but he suddenly seized her wrist. In one last effort he said earnestly, 'Are you sure you haven't heard anything about this mine disaster? This McArnot mine?'

'Larry,' she laid one hand softly on his wrist. 'If there had been such an accident I would know. It would be in all the papers. But I haven't read or heard anything about it. I can assure you that Rogart is no more than a crank.'

She tried to free her wrist then but he only gripped it more firmly. 'Is that what you really think, Nurse? Or do you think that I'm lying?'

Her voice remained mild. 'I don't think that at all. I merely think that Rogart was lying.'

'Then who tried to break in here?' His tone was savage.

'I don't know. Possibly it was all your imagination.'

He stared into her cool gaze, then bitterly he let her go.

Doubt flickered in her eyes for a moment, then she said quietly, 'Forget Rogart. There's nothing to worry about.' She smiled again then turned away to lock the windows. Without looking back at him she found a brush and pan and cleared up the broken remains of the vase on the floor. Then she picked up her coat and gave him a final professional smile. 'Good night, Larry. And stop worrying.'

He bade her a moody good night as she switched off the light and went out. It was a long time before he fell into a shallow, uneasy sleep.

★ ★ ★

The next morning the doctor came in to see him. He was undoubtedly angry at Rogart abusing his trust and added his own reassurances to those of the nurse. Rogart was again branded as a crank. When Larry brought up the question of his midnight visitor Howell seemed more dubious.

'Are you certain that someone did try to break in?' he asked.

'Quite certain.' Larry made an effort to remain calm.

Howell went on unabashed, 'Of course it's quite possible that what you heard was just the wind rustling the leaves, or a mouse scampering up the walls. Your imagination could have done the rest. You got up and rushed outside, and then chased shadows into the shrubbery.'

'There was no wind, and I wasn't chasing shadows.'

'Oh, well, I'll ask the watchman to keep a sharper eye open in future.'

With that Larry had to be satisfied. Howell was a good doctor, but he was obviously quite accustomed to disregarding the imaginations of his patients. Probably the majority of his cases were highly strung nervous disorders. It seemed that kind of place anyhow.

When Howell had gone Larry got up again and examined the french windows. There, in the clear light of day, a host of tiny scratches were visible in the edges of the lock. Something sharp had cut into the metal there when the door was forced open. For a moment he thought of ringing for the doctor or the nurse and pointing out the tell-tale marks. But he didn't. After the let-down the nurse had given him the previous night he was again wary of trusting anyone.

He passed the morning in useless

speculation, and after lunch the nurse brought him a dressing-gown and slippers and deposited him in a chair outside. The sun was warm and it made a break to get out of the bed. Two elderly men, both obvious nerve cases, kept him company.

Conversation with his fellow sufferers kept him occupied all afternoon, until at last a nurse came to take them in. As they left one of them offered him a newspaper he had finished reading. Larry accepted it with thanks and watched the man out of sight. Then he turned his attention to the paper. As he opened it out his body froze with sudden fear. The bold black lettering of the headlines seemed to spring up at his eyes and reverberate through his brain.

He read them slowly:

McARNOT MINE DISASTER —
STILL NO STATEMENT ON
MISSING SURVIVOR

The unidentified journalist who was pulled clear of the falling shaft in the McArnot mine disaster is still missing. It is now two days since this mystery man vanished from an ambulance that was rushing him to hospital. Described as young, approximately twenty-five years old, and known only by the name of Brown, this man is now the subject of a nationwide search. Several shots from a gun brought down the shaft as he was hauled up. The man was in a critically shocked state, his clothes torn and his face streaked with blood. How he has so far escaped capture in such a noticeable condition is a mystery.

Attempts are still going on to reach the three men still in the mine but there are no other entrances, the old shafts having caved in years ago. At the moment the police are excavating one of the blocked tunnels that connect the old workings with the modern pit nearby. They have little hope of finding the three men alive.

Larry read no further. He sat there stunned and the printed lines blurred before his eyes. His mind was unable to focus properly and nothing seemed real any more. Everything was confusion;

unanswerable questions; lies and intrigue. And the sense of it all was lost and buried in his unknown past. For a long time he was motionless and then the haze of shock began to clear, like the dust of a desert sandstorm dying after the wind has passed. It cleared and above it all rose one sharp question. Why had Nurse Denning lied?

Perhaps that was the most meaningless one of all, but it was the one he most wanted answered. He wondered why. Perhaps he was in love? But that was ridiculous. Falling in love with your nurse was like calf love, short-lived and mostly fond imagining. Something you got over as soon as you began to move about a bit.

With an effort he finally pushed the dark-haired nurse from his mind and tried to concentrate on the more important matters. He re-read the newspaper report, and though it did nothing to jog his memory he knew that he had to be that missing survivor. The nature of his injuries proved that, especially his face, streaked with deep scratches. The nurse had said they looked like claw marks from some large cat or bird. He wondered what there could be down the mine to have clawed his face like that?

Involuntarily he shivered.

He sat there for a long time, deep in thought. And when Nurse Denning eventually came out to take him back to his bed he hurriedly stuffed his newspaper in his pyjama jacket out of sight. Back in his room she helped him take off his dressing-gown, and while she turned her back to hang it up he transferred the paper swiftly to his bed. When she had gone he drew it out and read through the report a third time. The more he thought about it the more a vague idea hardened into grim resolve until he knew exactly what he had to do.

Somehow he had to find out what had happened in the depths of the old McArnot mine and whether or not he had been responsible for the deaths of the three men who had not returned. And why was the mysterious Mr. Rogart so concerned over whatever grim drama had been played out in the bowels of the earth?

And there was only one place where he might find the answers. Only one course of action that might bring back his memory and save his sanity — or even his neck. Somehow he had to break out of the nursing home, make his way north into Scotland, and then find some method of entry to the old McArnot mine.

★ ★ ★

By nightfall Larry's nerves were beginning to vibrate slightly from the tension of waiting. Once he had made up his mind to break out it seemed imperative that he should do so quickly. To delay might mean that the police would find a way into the mine before him, and that would spell disaster. How he intended to accomplish something that the police had spent several fruitless days trying to do, he didn't really know. He only knew he had to try. Apart from lying on his back and taking anything that might come, it was the only alternative.

He waited until well over an hour after 'lights out' before he made his move. To have left earlier might have meant bumping into a late-going member of the staff, while to leave later meant less time to get clear of the nursing home before his escape was discovered at dawn. He got out of bed silently and slipped his dressing-gown over his shoulders before moving to the door. Here he listened closely. So far he had seen no signs that the police were keeping any kind of guard on him, and the fact that no one had appeared when he chased his mystery visitor into the shrubbery the previous night seemed to prove they were not. But still he listened to be sure.

There was no sound of any description. Very gently he tried the door and inched it carefully open. There was no light in the corridor, and still nothing to be heard. He closed the door softly behind him, not wanting anyone to investigate an open door and discover his disappearance too soon. The longer the start he had, the better.

Turning left he padded silently up the corridor, counting doors as he went. The elderly man who had given him the newspaper was about the same height and build as he was, and occupied the room three french windows away from his own. It was there he meant to call for some clothes. He felt mean about stealing from a man who had befriended him, but he had to have clothes and he didn't want to blunder into some woman's room by mistake while searching for them. He counted three doors and then stopped.

Again he had to listen carefully, but there was no sound, either from inside the room or out. His fingers closed over the knob on the door and he realized abruptly that his hand was damp with sweat. He twisted slowly and pushed the door open a fraction at a time. There was still no sound.

He stepped into the room and pushed the door to behind him. Just a faint ray of moonlight was coming through a chink in the curtains but he could see nothing else. Then he heard the soft wheezing sound of a sleeper's breath, and placed the bed in a corresponding position to the one in his own room. With a silent prayer he acted on the assumption that the rest of the furniture would be similarly arranged and felt his way to where the wardrobe should be.

He found it, running his hands lightly over the polished wood with a feeling of relief. Quietly he opened it and felt inside. He found a suit on a hangar and a folded pile of clothes on the top shelf. There were a pair of shoes on the bottom. He gathered up the lot, closed the wardrobe, and made his way silently back to his own room.

He paused to get his breath back and then swiftly set about getting dressed. It was difficult in the dark, especially in alien clothes. He ripped a button off the shirt as he was putting it on and then climbed into the trousers back to front. He swore softly and started again. Succeeding at last he finally put on the shoes. They were a little large but he made then fit comfortably by padding the toes with strips of his pyjamas. Then at last he was ready to leave.

He crossed to the french windows and pushed through the curtains. The lawn outside was deserted. There was no life anywhere. With a brief prayer he unlocked the door and stepped outside. There was no point in hesitating now and after a swift glance round he sprinted for the shadows of the shrubbery. Looking back he saw that the whole building was in complete darkness. The night was cold and the moon bright in a cloudy sky. It was a full moon and he waited for it to slide behind the ragged edges of a cloud-bank before moving on.

The soft earth made no sound beneath his feet and he tried to avoid rustling the leaves as he went. He followed the same route he had taken the previous night and came out again on the drive facing the birch copse. The moon reappeared for a few seconds and danced on the silvery trunks of the trees, then it vanished and they were just faint white streaks in the gloom. He hurried away from the black outline of the house, keeping close to the shadows of the shrubbery. There was no sound but the vague scuffling of his feet

75

in the gravel. The drive curved gradually in a slow S bend and he followed it closely, eyes and ears alert. Once he thought he heard a sound behind him but he dismissed it as imagination. It was easy to imagine things in circumstances like this. Then he saw a pair of high, wrought-iron, gates ahead, and beside them, to the left of the drive, a small wooden hut.

He moved even more cautiously from there, wondering if the nightwatchman would be in or whether he had rounds to make. He kept well in the shrubbery and approached the place from behind. His heart was beginning to speed up again and the tension tightened its grip. He reached the side wall of the hut and moved with his back to it round the edge. There was a small window by his left shoulder and on the other side of that the door. He peered cautiously through the window and then the tension left him like air from a shrinking balloon. The nightwatchman sprawled back in his chair, old and fat and fast asleep.

Larry smiled to himself and moved

past the hut to the gates. There was a small side gate beside the main ones and it was partly open. He squeezed through without opening it further, just in case it should creak. Ten yards beyond, the gravel ended on a tarmac road and he turned sharp right and hurried away.

It was then that he heard steps behind him, scuffling hurriedly through the last of the gravel and then bursting into a run along the road. He hesitated, torn between fight and flight. If he ran the hunt was up, if he fought he might gain a few more hours. The running steps were right behind him when he whirled sharply. If he could knock out the nightwatchman he had a chance yet.

But it wasn't the nightwatchman. It was Nurse Denning again.

5

Who Is Crane?

Larry checked the blow he was about to aim, his fist faltering half way through its swing. He recoiled a step, letting his bunched fist drop to his side. A man he could have hit but not the nurse. She came on unhesitatingly and lunged forward to grab at the lapels of his stolen jacket. Her face was strained and breathless and she almost fell into him. The brown eyes were wildly angry and for a few moments she was unable to speak.

Those few moments seemed to last an eternity. Larry felt lost and baffled, cursing the filthy luck that had caused him to again be caught by the nurse. If only it had been a man he could have silenced him with a knock-out blow and still given himself a few hours' start. But he couldn't hit a woman, least of all the dark-haired nurse. He could only stand there helplessly, waiting for her to speak.

She was wearing the same wide collared grey coat. It hung open to reveal a dark skirt and a red silk blouse. The blouse heaved steadily as she sucked in her breath. Her dark curls were awry and she was angry. She glared at him furiously, both hands clenched around the lapels of his jacket and the small knuckles showing white.

'What the hell do you think you're playing at?' she panted at last, the words jerking out erratically as she struggled for breath. 'Somehow I — I knew it was you when I saw you slipping along — ' she gulped another mouthful of air ' — along the drive.'

The sound of her voice seemed to inject life into his uncertain limbs again. He couldn't hit her but at least he didn't have to let her hold him. His hands came up and clamped over her slim wrists and he exerted all his strength in a downward wrench that tore her hands away from his jacket.

'I'm sorry, nurse, but I'm leaving.' He thrust her away from him, turned around and ran.

'Come back here!' She yelled the words after him as she staggered back on her heels. Then, regaining her balance, she sprinted after him.

Larry heard the clatter of her heels on the road behind him and increased his pace to the utmost. He drew away from her, hearing the sound of her footsteps fade. But his chest was already straining and he couldn't keep it up. The nurse kept on doggedly behind him and then when he slowed began to close the gap.

Larry heard her coming up again and put on another spurt, but this time it was even shorter. The days in bed had left him stiff with his muscles all gummed together, and now he couldn't loosen up into a proper stride. The nurse hadn't wasted any breath on calling to him after that first shout and the sound of her feet drew ever nearer.

They covered nearly two hundred yards of the deserted, unlit, road. Passing the high wall that circled the nursing home grounds, and then on past a few isolated cottages. Then abruptly the nurse put on an unexpected sprint. Larry heard her right behind him and tried to break into a third spurt. His legs seemed to get crossed and he almost fell, and then her hand clutched at his shoulder, slithering and groping down his back, and finally closing on the tail of his jacket. She dragged him to a halt and flung one arm around him like a wrestler groping for a hold.

Larry whirled round, struggling to free himself as she hung on with the tenacity of a bulldog. He twisted in her arms and tried to push her away, almost succeeding before she changed her grip and got a hold on his jacket again. He panted and writhed, wrenching his bad arm as he wrestled frantically in her grasp. And then suddenly fear filled him. Blind, unreasoning, fear that was born deep in his stomach and swelled like a growing monster through his body. It sent spear heads of terror shrieking along the tightened wires of his nerves, rising and blotting out all coherent thought until his mind became a complete blank. Without knowing he was lashing out savagely, his bunched fists flailing wildly in a desperate surge of panic. One vicious blow landed with a ringing crack on the side of the nurse's smashing her aside. She fell senseless to the ground.

He came out of his black-out in a daze. Bewildered and frightened and ashamed by the unexpected violence that lay within him. He had to shake his head to clear the fog that obscured his brain, it was like coming round after a drugged sleep, knowing that something had happened but being unsure what. It took a few moments for the numbness to release its grip on his mind and then for the first time he knew what he had done.

She lay on her back, her coat rumpled and creased around her. Her breasts were lifting slowly beneath the silk blouse and there was already an ugly, bluish, bruise beginning to show on the neat line of her jaw. Her eyes were closed and her dark head resting in the dirt on the side of the road.

Larry knelt beside her slowly, afraid

of what he had done. He hadn't meant to hit her. That was why he had ran, because he didn't think it was possible that he could knock her down. But he had hit her. Some sleeping power of violence deep inside him had reared up to smash her down. It made him afraid, sick and trembling as he knelt by the roadside. If he could black out and do this to a young girl who was merely trying in her own way to help him, what might he have done to those three men in the mine?

He lifted her head slowly, resting her shoulders on his knees with his arm behind her neck. The dark head lolled back over his arm, the bruise on her jaw showing clear against the white of her face and the taut lines of her throat. He lifted her a little higher and very gently felt around the bruise with his fingers. With a sense of relief he decided that nothing was broken. If he had hit her smack on the point of the jaw he would probably have broken the bone, but as it was the blow had landed just to the side.

For a long time he knelt in the road, looking down at her. She seemed very frail and helpless as she lay limp in his arms, more of a sleeping child now than the efficient, capable nurse. He began to wonder what he was going to do with her then. He could hardly leave her lying by the roadside. She might lie undiscovered for hours and perhaps die of the cold and exposure. There were a lot of unpleasant things that could happen to a defenceless girl lying unconscious on the roadside.

He realized suddenly that he had to make his decision fast, for he was still within a stone's throw of the last few cottages they had run past. They were all in darkness but it was still a dangerous place to linger. He had to get away. He made up his mind swiftly then. Until he could find somewhere safe to leave her, he was taking her with him. Crazy as it was, he was taking her with him. He felt terribly responsible for her safety now that he had struck her down.

Determinedly he thrust his free arm beneath her knees and gathered her up in his arms as he got to his feet. He turned his back to the nursing home and set off at a brisk walk. It was very dark now, for the moon had vanished behind a rolling mass of cloud. He had the impression that he was passing through some fields and woods, and then after a while he came to a crossroads. There was a signpost but he didn't bother to read it, he simply turned north.

The time passed and the girl grew heavy in his arms. Several times he had to dive for cover in the ditch beside the road as cars shot past, crouching low over the girl as the beam of the headlights swept overhead. Finally, after it seemed he had been walking for hours, he came upon a white metal sign that told him he was now entering the village of Sturwell.

He moved more warily then. It was risky to pass through a village with the limp girl in his arms, but he had to keep going. He only hoped that everyone would be asleep. A light showed up ahead and he took the precaution of crossing to the far side of the road. As he drew nearer he realized that the lights were those of a café and that before it were parked two large lorries.

He stopped. An all night café was an unexpected surprise on this road, but the lorries were a gift from heaven, both were facing north. He made up his mind in an instant and closed in on the café.

Inside he could see two men, obviously the lorry drivers, sitting at a corner table. A blonde waitress was smiling and leaning over them, revelling in the interest they paid to her low-cut neckline. One of the men was trying to pinch her seat and she was slapping his hand down without backing away. Larry smiled and blessed her. Swiftly he unfastened the straps on the canvas hood at the back of the nearest lorry and bundled Nurse Denning into the back. He shot another glance at the windows where the giggling waitress still flirted with the two men, blessed her again, and then swung up into the lorry. Carefully he drew the flaps together again.

At the front end of the lorry was a high load of packing cases, but at the back was a few feet of clear space. Here Larry made himself comfortable and settled down to wait. He lifted the girl so that her head and shoulders were cradled in his arms. Her face was a white smudge in the darkness and he had to listen for the soft sound of her breathing to reassure himself that she was still alive. He still didn't know what he was going to do with her. He thought vaguely of leaving her near the café where she would be found quickly. But obviously whoever found her would instantly call a doctor to revive her, and then the hunt would be on for him. Again he had to resign himself to the inevitable. The only way to see she came to no harm, and at the same time not set the police on his trail was to keep her with him.

He had to wait half an hour before the two drivers finally left the café, still laughing with the waitress as they climbed into their cabs. A few moments later they were away.

Once clear of the café Larry relaxed. He opened the flaps to watch the hedgrows flash past and tried to plot out his next move. He had no delusions about the task he had set himself. His white swathed face made him a marked man, and by dawn every policeman in the country would be out looking for him. That was his biggest obstacle, unless he hid by day and moved only at night the first person to see him would recognize his glaring white face.

For a while a lethargy of despair settled upon him. The odds were stacked against him. He still had the unconscious nurse on his hands, and even if he reached the mine he would still have to find a way into the old galleries.

With an effort he pushed those moments of despair behind him. It would be a good game to win he told himself. All he needed was a smile from lady luck and he could bluff his way through. It was a challenge, but it would be a good game to win.

He quit worrying then, and began watching the road signs as the lorry travelled north. They were moving fast up the A161 and finally joined the A19 before entering the city of York. They had to slow as they went through the silent streets, and past the old Roman walls.

Once clear of the city again Larry decided that he would have to leave the lorry at the first chance he got for he had to be in hiding by dawn. Daylight would be his worst enemy now. Slowly the tension began to build up inside him as he waited for his opportunity. But the lorry still cruised effortlessly up the A19 and showed no signs of stopping.

Larry began to sweat with the nagging fear that the driver might carry on without stopping until well after dawn when it would be too late for him to escape unseen. Despair began to close in again and this time took a greater effort to fight off. He had to remind himself that the driver had been going for over three hours now and at any time must surely stop. No driver risked fatigue and accidents by carrying on too long.

When the lorry did eventually slow down it startled him. The vehicle jerked as the driver changed gear, and Larry cautiously pulled open the flaps in readiness. The lorry pulled into a lay by. Larry heard the cab door slam as the driver got out and for a moment he thought that the man must have become suspicious and was coming round the back. He began to sweat a little, but the driver merely hummed to himself and stayed up near the front. With a surge of relief Larry realized that the man was only obeying the call of nature.

He waited until the man re-entered his cab again then swiftly dropped out on to the road. He hoisted up the girl's inert body, and was only just in time to get her out as the lorry pulled away. He watched it disappear before taking stock of his surroundings.

Up ahead was a small cluster of farm buildings lying well off the road. Behind them was a copse of small trees. Briskly he started towards them, knowing that by dawn he had to be under cover. With his face so distinctively swathed in bandages he hadn't a hope of remaining undetected in the open.

With the unconscious girl in his arms, he passed the rough track that led to the farm and carried on until the copse was between him and the buildings. A quick glance round and he stepped over the low wire fence and into the woods, circling back to the farm through the trees.

Low branches plucked at him as he moved through the wrinkled boles, his feet swishing softly in the grass. A twig snapped loudly beneath his heel and his mouth dried up again. Then suddenly he saw the outline of a barn, set ideally in the trees some fifty yards away from the house. It was the sort of thing he was hoping for and he changed course towards it.

He kept one eye constantly on the main buildings as he approached the barn, but there was no signs of life to alarm him. The trees were thinner here and he quickened his pace. He didn't like this open stretch. He almost ran the last few paces to the side of the barn, and stood there in the dense shadows with his chest heaving and his mouth even drier than before.

He paused for a few seconds to listen and then moved warily around to the front of the barn. A muddy track led up to the farmyard and the farmhouse but there was still no signs of life in that direction. He turned to the barn doors then, large double doors that were secured by a single wooden bar. Letting go of the girl's legs he held her with one arm while he used the other to lift the bar out of its slots. The bar was heavy and it was a feat of strength to lift it with one hand. He felt as though his arm would crack as he lifted down an end at a time.

Swiftly he pulled open one of the doors and lifted his burden inside. Another quick glance at the silent farm buildings and he closed the door behind him, praying that the farmer would not notice that it was unbarred.

It was pitch dark in the barn but after a few minutes of groping around he managed to stumble on a heap of straw. And settling the girl beside him he relaxed weakly on his back. It was then that she stirred.

He sat up again, staring at, but not seeing her in the darkness. She moved again and he began to gently tap her face to bring her round. For the moment the big problem of what to do with her was no longer in his mind. All he wanted was to hear her voice again; to know that he had not caused her any lasting harm.

She began to moan a little as she came round and he lifted her upright, still lightly slapping her face. She moaned louder and her hand groped up weakly to check his slapping. He remembered her bruised jaw and stopped.

'Nurse Denning,' he whispered urgently. 'Nurse Denning, are you okay?'

There was silence, then her voice came weak and bewildered. 'Larry, Larry, what happened?'

'I hit you,' he said simply. 'I don't know why. I didn't want to — I didn't mean to. I just lost my head somehow and hit you.'

Again there was silence. And he sensed by her movements that she was gently feeling her jaw. Then abruptly she asked a strange question.

'Larry, who is Crane?'

For a moment he was startled. He searched his mind for an answer yet didn't even understand the question. At last he said, 'I don't know, the name means nothing.'

Her hand found his shoulder in the darkness and closed on it gently.

'You should Larry.' Her voice was soft but serious. 'Crane is the man you were fighting. You blacked out and you were mentally re-living that fight with him when you hit me. Just before I went out you were screaming. You said: 'No Crane! Crane, you crazy swine!' Those were your exact words.'

Larry felt lost, the feeling of defeat sweeping over him again. The questions kept piling up and there were never any answers. Who was Crane?

6

'We Go Together'

To Larry that new question was like the final straw that broke the camel's back. There were so many questions with missing answers that another one had the effect of crumbling his resistance into utter ruin. He was getting nowhere. Every step he took was bringing him face to face with more questions — more problems. It was like walking out into a swamp and feeling the mud build up around him, sucking him down until it closed over his head and engulfed him forever. Down and down into the endless morass of questions that had no answer.

Nurse Denning sensed something of his feelings for her hand stayed firm on his shoulder. She said nothing but her presence and the soft weight of her hand caused him to clench his teeth

95

as he fought off the lurking threat of despair. It was as if she was willing hope into his mind from her own, guiding it through the contact of her hand on his shoulder. He could see nothing of her face in the darkness but knew she was looking up into his own. Gradually he began to feel the new confidence she had instilled within him seeping through his body. And with it came the return of grim determination. What was another question to him? It was just another cloud in the storm; another spash of water in the sea. He told himself that it was still a good game to win. That was his motto now, his catch phrase — his password to success. It was a good game to win.

After a while he said quietly, 'I'm still sorry I hit you.'

'You didn't hit me,' she told him gently. 'You hit a man named Crane. I just happened to be there in his place.' She hesitated a moment then asked. 'Are you sure the name means nothing to you, Larry?'

He shook his head, a pointless gesture

in the darkness. 'No. I can't remember ever hearing the name before, much less fighting with the man.'

'Well it's obvious you did. Somewhere in your past you fought him. And it must have been a pretty terrible fight for you to re-live it the way you did. You were afraid when you knocked me down, Larry. Terribly afraid. You were lashing out in blind panic. You weren't even seeing me. Your mind held someone else.'

'I'm still sorry,' he faltered weakly. 'How's your jaw?'

'Throbbing like blazes.' She winced slightly as she touched it in the darkness. 'You pack quite a punch.'

'I guess so, you were out a long time.'

She started abruptly as he spoke and as her body brushed against him he felt a tingle of alarm run through her limbs. He felt her go tense beside him and then she said slowly, 'Where are we, Larry?'

'In a barn.' He felt helpless again, unsure what to do next. 'You've no need to be alarmed. I only brought you

97

because — because I just couldn't sling you in the hedge and leave you. I didn't want to hurt you any more.'

He knew she was looking at him when she said evenly, 'Well, Larry — are you going to walk back to the nursing home with me?'

'You don't understand.' She had taken her hand from his shoulder and a little of his new found confidence had gone with it. 'We're no longer near the nursing home. We're over a hundred miles away, on the other side of York.'

'York!' she repeated the word incredulously. 'But why, Larry? What are you trying to do?'

'I'm heading north, to Scotland. I got this far by hiding in the back of a lorry. You've been out for several hours. It must be near dawn now, so I took cover for the day.'

She was silent for a moment. Analysing his words carefully to make quite clear of his meaning. Then she asked, 'And what about me?'

'I don't know.' He spread his hands vaguely, oblivious of the fact that she could not see them. 'I kept trying to think of some way to leave you somewhere safe and still give myself a few hours' start. But it just wasn't possible. I couldn't just dump you either. You might have caught pneumonia or died of exposure or something. The ground was damp everywhere.'

'And now you still don't know what to do with me?'

'No, I kept thinking that something would turn up, but it didn't. Now — well, perhaps I can tie you up or something. You should be safe enough in here. It's warm and dry. And you can kick things around, make a noise like that to attract attention when someone comes near. You shouldn't be here for more than a few hours.'

'And what about you?'

'I'll move on, see if I can get clear of this district and lie low again before dawn. It's still pitch dark so I've probably got another hour or so.'

She was silent again, sitting thoughtfully beside him on the straw. When she spoke her voice was still quiet and even.

'Supposing I shout and scream when you start to tie me up, what then?'

'I — I guess I don't know.' He felt helpless again. 'Will you?'

Her hand found his arm and closed over it. Perhaps it was a gesture of restraint but he didn't think so. It was eerie talking to a quiet even voice in the pitch blackness. The whole conversation seemed weird and unreal, it wasn't taking place the way such a conversation should have done. He believed that she sensed it too. That she needed that slight reassurance of human contact to prove she was not talking in a dream.

She finally answered him, her tone still calm. 'No, at least I don't intend to scream yet. First I want to know why. Why are you running away? What you're running away from?'

'I'm not running from anything. I just realized that I was getting nowhere by staying where I was. If I wanted to know things, then I had to go out and find them out for myself. Staying in bed wasn't the way to learn the answers.'

'What sort of answers? To what sort of things?'

He remembered that she had lied and hesitated, then said coldly, 'Like what happened down the old McArnot mine. I read a newspaper report that confirmed everything Rogart said.'

She said nothing and he knew that she too was remembering how she had lied about the existence of the mine. He wanted to ask her why. It was terribly important to him that he found out just why she had lied. But he couldn't ask. Somehow he just couldn't. He had to wait and hope that she would tell him. The darkness in the old barn seemed to tighten around them, the straw rustled as she moved uncomfortably. A sharp stalk scratched his leg but he ignored it, waiting for her to speak.

'I'm sorry I had to lie to you, Larry.' She let the words out slowly. Weighing each one carefully before she used it. 'You see it was on Doctor Howell's instructions. He believed that you had been subjected to some kind of ghastly ordeal down that mine. Something so horrible that you didn't want to remember it — a kind of self-induced amnesia. Whatever happened to your face, Larry, it wasn't caused when that shaft caved in around you, something ripped your face into a mess before that.' She paused for a few moments to select her next words, and went on: 'Doctor Howell believed that to confront you with what few facts we knew too quickly would only force the memory of what happened further into your subconscious mind. He wanted to give you time to recover before he began to probe into your past. A bad psychological shock is like a raw wound. If you rush in clumsily you can do more harm than good. It has to be treated carefully.'

'Then I take it that Howell is a psychologist?'

'That's right. His patients are all nervous disorders or convalescents. Anyway, he insisted that at first you were to be told as little as possible. He was mad at the police for worrying you but they were equally insistent on satisfying themselves that you were in fact suffering from amnesia, and not swinging the lead. Inspector James was actually a police psychiatrist. They were satisfied and consented to leave you in the doctor's hands. They said nothing to the newspapers because they didn't want anyone worrying you.'

Larry frowned. 'If that's so, how did that Mr. Rogart get in?'

'He said he believed you might be a relation of his who had disappeared in the district on the night you were found. How he discovered your whereabouts I don't really know. He said he had just heard about you, and Doctor Howell thought that one of the staff had been talking. He was very wild about it. However he talked to Rogart and saw no reason to disbelieve the man. And although he posed some leading questions Rogart gave no signs of knowing anything about the mine. The doctor thought it over and came to the opinion that it couldn't do any harm. He didn't think Rogart would be able to tell you anything he didn't want you to know, and there was always the chance that you might turn out to be his missing relative. The police wouldn't have allowed it of course, but Doctor Howell is the kind of man who would always put the interests of his patients first. He was terribly angry when I told him how Rogart had fooled him and what the man had told you. I told him I had denied the story and he agreed that that was the best way. He thought that despite Rogart you still might react better later on if you were given more time.'

She stopped there but Larry did not press her for more. For a few moments he needed time to think. Time to absorb all that she had told him and straighten it out in his mind. He tried to arrange his thoughts neatly but it was like building a house of cards, every few seconds they would come tumbling down in disorder again. But he didn't really care. Above them all one fact always stood out clearly. She had only lied for his own good; because she thought it would be best for him. It made him light-headed and free inside, as if all the other things didn't matter.

She went on suddenly: 'Of course we never expected you to run away like this.

Neither did the police. While you didn't remember anything you had no reason to run away.'

'No.' His tone was bitter. 'But now I have.'

Her hand closed more firmly about his arm. 'Why have you?'

'I should have thought it was obvious. There are so many things I have to know, and that old mine is the only place where I might find the answers.'

She said quietly, 'Why not be patient, Larry? The police are still trying to break into that old mine. Any time now they'll get through. They'll find all the answers for you. Why not come back with me to the nursing home and wait?'

'But supposing they think I did kill those three men, they'll hang me for murder.'

'Do you think you did, Larry?'

'I don't know.' There was a note of anguish in his tone. 'I don't know but — but I've got to find out. Don't you see — it's not the kind of thing I could take another man's word for. I've got to find out for myself.'

She twisted around in the straw to face him, her other hand closing on his other arm. It was his bad arm and her fingers hurt but she didn't notice. He was only just aware of it himself. She said earnestly, 'I don't think you did, Larry. The kind of man who could shoot three men down in cold blood wouldn't worry about slinging an unconscious nurse into a ditch. I don't think you could have done it.'

He said slowly, 'Neither do I. But I didn't think I could knock down a woman either until I smashed you senseless in a black-out. I might have had a black-out down there.'

'No, Larry.' Her words were insistent. 'You weren't fighting me. You were fighting a man named Crane. At least that's what you thought you were doing. I've explained that.'

'Perhaps I thought I was shooting someone else when I shot those three men.'

'*If* you shot them.'

'What else could I have shot at down

there? There were three shots, and three bullets — '

'That proves nothing, Larry. It was just coincidence. It — '

'Listen!' the sharpness of the word cut her silent. 'Listen a minute. I was the last man out of that mine. The police are certain of it. So was Rogart. So are you and Howell. And I'm certain of it too. It just has to be that way. There are too many coincidences for it to be wrong. So, don't you see? I've got to know what happened down there. I've got to see for myself. Otherwise I shall drive myself crazy.'

She was silent for a moment, then she said softly, 'I can understand. But it's so hopeless. Even if you reach the mine, how do you expect to find a way in before the police? If they can't do it how can you?'

'I don't know.' He laughed bitterly. 'That's beginning to be my life story: I don't know. But I've got to try all the same.'

'Yes,' she breathed slowly. 'I suppose you have.'

'It's my only way. If the police catch me, or I go back, then nothing changes. My only way out is to go on.' He paused there for a moment, and then abruptly clamped his hand over her wrist and demanded: 'Suppose it does work out that I killed those men? What then? What will it mean — to you?'

'You're not capable of murder, Larry. Even if you can't be sure, I am.' Her tone said as much as the words themselves.

He felt the tension leave him then and slowly released her wrist. She remained silent for a while, giving him time to think over his position. Then she asked calmly, 'Are you sure you won't reconsider? Leave it to the police and come back with me.'

'I can't do it that way. I thought I'd made you understand.'

'Then you're back very near to where we started, aren't you? What are you going to do with me?'

The question jerked his mind back to his first problem. He had almost forgotten that theoretically she was still on the side of the law. It startled him and for a moment he couldn't think. What was he going to do? What could he do?

She went on seriously, 'How far do you really think you'll get, Larry? By morning every police force in the country will be on the lookout for you. And by the time the evening papers come out tonight there won't be a man or woman in the British Isles who won't recognize you on sight. Your bandaged face makes you a marked man. You don't stand a chance.'

'I'll hide by day, and travel only by night.' The sudden defiance in his voice surprised him.

'You won't get far. You've only got to be seen once and the game will be up. The police will concentrate their search and bring you in within an hour.'

'It's as good a chance as going back. And I'm taking it.' He was staring towards her. The calm way she put her arguments gave no clue as to what was in her mind, and he was wishing he could see into those large brown eyes.

'Your luck can't last, Larry. The odds are too great.'

'I'm still going to try.'

'Then I can't talk you out of it? Whatever happens you're determined to go it alone?'

He said shortly, 'Yes.'

She hesitated the barest fraction of a second, then said firmly, 'Then I'm coming with you.'

For a moment he couldn't think of a rely. Anything else and a retort would have been ready on his tongue, but that short statement left him baffled. He stammered slowly, 'But you can't do that. You can't.'

'Don't be a fool, Larry. You'll never get through alone. The moment you show your face in public you'll be picked up before you move a dozen yards. On your own you just can't make it, but if I help you, you just might.'

'Why?' For the moment it was all he could think of. 'Why?'

'I don't know really.' Her tone was quiet and uncertain. 'When I first started you talking, I meant to talk you into going back. But now I realize that that's useless and it seems criminal to let you go alone. I still think you should go back. But if you've got to go, then we'll go together.'

She stirred in the straw and this time he felt the pressure of her body as she moved in beside him. Her hand found his and then his other hand strayed, half frightened, to touch her shoulder.

He said grimly, as grimly as he could: 'I still might be a murderer, Nurse. You might be helping the wrong kind of man. You've got to think of that.'

'I've thought.' Her voice was very close now. 'And I don't believe it's possible. That's why I'm going along.'

He wanted to kiss her suddenly, but he didn't. This was madness. He couldn't involve her in this mess. It was unfair. He had nothing to lose, but she had plenty. Her reputation, her job, perhaps even her freedom. Helping a murderer escape was a criminal offence. If he was a murderer. And even if he wasn't he was still a wanted man, or would be as soon as the police knew of his escape. It amounted to the same thing.

He said firmly, 'Thanks for the offer, Nurse, but it won't do. All I'm asking is that you give me a few hours' start. I've got you into enough trouble already.'

'Larry, I mean it. If you have to go on then I'm coming with you. Otherwise you might as well come back to the nursing home.'

'I'm doing neither. I'm going alone.'

'You're not, you're going with me. Don't worry. I can't get into any serious trouble.'

'You'll be helping a wanted man.'

'But you haven't been charged with anything yet.'

'Yet,' he repeated gloomily.

He sensed her smiling again in the darkness as she went on. 'Besides, you're going to need a nurse to look after you. Without me to keep an eye on them you'll probably let those cuts go septic.'

He made no answer and she squeezed his hand gently. Again he wished that he could see her in the darkness. Somehow he felt that it would help him to make up his mind. His brain was awhirl with all the advantages and disadvantages, and above them all was the clear fact that he didn't want her involved. The presence of the mysterious Rogart indicated that there was more to the puzzle around the mine disaster than he might have thought. He had the feeling that danger would lurk along the way and he didn't want her harmed.

Her fingers kept up their steady pressure on his hand and slowly the realization sank in that she was right. Alone he wouldn't stand a chance.

He said quietly, 'If you're coming with me I think I ought to know your name.'

'It's Linda — Linda Denning.' She squeezed his hand. 'Now let's get some sleep, Larry. It'll be dawn soon and you must be tired.'

7

On The Run

Larry was barely asleep when Linda shook him sharply into consciousness. He became aware of her urgent hands gripping his shoulders and the fact that his back was arched uncomfortably in the straw. He stirred, straightening himself out and shaking his head dazedly. It was faintly light and he saw her looking down at him. He tried to open his mouth to speak but her hand clamped suddenly over his lips.

'Shhh, listen.' It was hardly a whisper.

He lay still, sensing the tension in her as she knelt over him. The pressure of her hand on his mouth relaxed slightly but he only moved his eyes. It was dawn. The plank walls of the old barn were far from flush and countless thin lines of light streaked the dusty floor. He listened, and then he heard the sound that had

114

alarmed her. A low, throaty, growl that rose abruptly to an angry bark. It was a dog.

The animal barked louder, deep throated snarls of displeasure. It sounded a fairly large sized brute and Larry cursed himself mentally. Every farmyard had a dog. He should have realized that. To hide near a farm where there would be dogs sniffing about was simply asking to be caught. The dog disrupted the silence with another fit of barking. He was trying to judge the distance now and it seemed that the dog was some distance away still. Probably near the house.

He removed Linda's hand slowly from his mouth and sat up in the straw. There were plenty of cracks and knot-holes in the doors of the barn and he rose up silently and crossed towards them. Kneeling before the largest he peered through and up the muddy track towards the farm. He could see a lot clearer now that it was daylight. The track passed through an open gate to a wide yard that ended against the back of the farmhouse. The building had a cosy look about it with its thatched roof and red brick chimneys. The curtains were all drawn at the windows. On the two sides of the yard were long low-roofed sheds. And in the far corner near the house was a large dog kennel with a hefty Alsatian straining at the chain.

The Alsatian was young but fully grown, its roughened coat grey and metallic looking in the dawn. It rattled the steel chain and kept up its barking until the back door of the farmhouse opened and the farmer came out to release it.

Linda knelt down by Larry and watched as the farmer unhooked the chain from the dog's collar. She said slowly: 'Do you think he knows we're here?'

Larry slipped his arm round her shoulders. 'I doubt it, he just wants to be let off. If he was a good watch dog he would have heard us last night and barked the place down.'

They watched as the Alsatian scurried around in a fast circle that brought it back to its master's feet. It yelped eagerly and then shot away in a wider circle. 'Noisy ow devil,' said the farmer amiably. Then he turned and went back inside.

The Alsatian raced up to the closed door and then stopped with its tongue lolling out. It wagged its tail eagerly and then scampered around the yard again. Larry watched it exhaust itself and then said softly:

'See what I mean. He's not coming this way at all.'

'No,' she admitted dubiously. 'He isn't.'

They watched the dog sniff around the yard. The animal was totally unaware of their presence, its nose down to the earth and the tail giving slight wriggles every few seconds. It explored all around the back of the farmhouse and then nosed its way into the long shed on the right hand side of the yard. It was out of sight for several moments and then a sudden pandemonium of yelps and squawks ended with it erupting out of the nearer end of the shed on the trail of a pair of flying chickens. It stopped there and eyed the indignant hens almost apologetically. They eyed him back before settling their ruffled feathers and strutting away. The dog lost interest and wandered over to inspect the gateposts.

In the barn both Larry and Linda held their breath as the Alsatian's ramblings brought it gradually nearer. It spent an eternity examining the gatepost before finally deciding to make use of it. Then it routed out a pheasant, a sleek and colourful cock bird that flew up screeching from the grass. It led him in a quick chase into the woods and from there it was out of sight.

They waited for the dog to return, more edgy than ever now that it was out of sight. The barking as it chased the fleeing pheasant through the trees died, and the sudden quiet held a silent note of menace. Larry felt Linda lean closer to him, reassured by human contact. He let his arm tighten gently around her shoulders.

They waited for long minutes before they finally spotted the Alsatian again.

He was suddenly very close, standing over to their left barely fifteen yards away. He stood there motionless, a silent grey threat with his head cocked and ears alert. Larry realized abruptly that the animal had crossed their trail; the path he had taken through the trees last night. It was suspicious now, it began to pad in closer, very cautious and completely silent.

They held their breath again. Larry bitterly cursing fate and the stray pheasant that had led the gambolling overgrown pup across their tracks.

The Alsatian came within two yards of the door. Meeting their eyes through the knothole. He squatted on his haunches, puzzled. Then he barked.

For a moment Larry thought of making a run for it. The dog was young and hardly looked dangerous. It was obviously a poor farm dog and barely trained. With luck it would merely scamper along beside them before tiring and turning away. Then, before he could put the idea to Linda, the back door of the farmhouse opened and the farmer strode out into the yard. This time he wore his jacket and a hat.

The Alsatian looked back and barked loudly. It got to its feet and then took a step nearer the barn. The barking changed to a surly growling in the deep throat.

' 'ere, 'ere yuh crerzy devil.'

The farmer called it once then turned into the shed where the chickens had been. The Alsatian stopped growling and looked over its shoulder. The brute looked as though it couldn't quite believe its ears, and the effect might have been funny except that the fugitives were rigid with suspense.

The farmer reappeared with a pail in each hand and started across the yard towards them. The dog emitted another series of growls and glared back at the barn. The farmer reached the gate and paused, the pails dragging at his arms.

'C'mon, what th' 'ell's a matter?'

The Alsatian barked furiously and lunged its jaws at the door. The sudden closeup view of angry eyes and teeth made Linda recoil and fall backwards on the floor, dragging Larry down with her. They lay sprawling with the Alsatian snarling at them through the knot holes.

' 'ere yuh crerzy 'ound, tha's nay rats in thar.'

The dog barked again and then the man yelled at it angrily to come to heel. It growled and they heard it shuffle about on the other side of the door. Another angry command and it moved away. They heard it bark again but the sound was receding. It died away as the dog moved off reluctantly after its owner. On the floor of the barn Larry found Linda looking into his eyes with a mixture of doubt and relief. She still couldn't quite believe it. Neither did he.

Larry got up at last and helped her to her feet. Her face was pale and she was breathing quickly. He said thankfully:

'Lady Luck was with us again. If that had been a reliable dog, that farmer would have been in here to see what it was all about. As it was the brute's young and scatterbrained and he didn't give its antics a second thought.'

Linda had recovered her composure a

little and began smoothing the creases out of her grey coat. She brushed the dust away and then asked quietly, 'What now, Larry? What do we do now?'

He frowned. 'Well it's obvious that we can't stay here, like I intended. When he gets back from feeding the hens, or wherever he's gone, that dog will be right back again. Eventually he must get suspicious and then our number will be up. The only thing to do is to get out of here and try to find some other cover for the rest of the day.'

She nodded slowly and he absently-minded picked a straw out of her dark hair. She patted her curls into place with one hand and then gazed vacantly around the barn. There was plenty of light now, streaming through chinks in the roof and the badly fitted boards. A solid square of it beamed through some panes of dirty glass high in the wall. They saw that the barn was little more than an old junk room. An ancient tractor was parked in one corner, almost hidden beneath a pile of old carpets and odd lengths of linoleum. Scraps of harness and rusting tools hung on the walls. There was an old tin trunk and a few articles of worm-eaten furniture, even an ancient grand piano with a splintered lid. Above them was a loft that covered only half the floor area, it was supported by wide-spaced poles along the centre of the barn and reached by a ladder. Nearby was the mound of straw where they had slept the night.

Linda said hesitantly, 'Let's take a look round. There's no telling what we might find that could be useful.'

Larry eyed their surroundings thoughtfully. She was right. Those old trunks might contain anything. A knife of some kind could be an invaluable help. If he was liable to meet up with Rogart again he felt he might need a weapon of some sort. A gun would have been ideal but that was too much to hope for. But a knife was possible.

'All right,' he agreed. 'We'll take a quick look round.'

They converged on the tin trunk and after an effort heaved open the rusted lid. The trunk was stacked high with old books and newspapers.

Linda eyed it mournfully. 'No luck there, I did think it might contain old clothes. I was hoping for a hat of some kind you could pull down over your face. It would serve to hide your bandages at a distance.'

Larry shrugged and shut the trunk. 'Let's look further.' He wandered away from her, kicking over old farming implements and upsetting a box of nails. She searched over towards the far side of the barn as he shifted the carpets on the tractor. He stepped back towards the centre of the barn and eyed the loft. He could make out some tea chests and climbed up slowly towards them. They were filled with junk, old toys and dust covered pictures in frames. The last one held old clothes but there was no hat. Mostly it was women's stuff, out-dated and waiting for a rag man. He started down the ladder again, telling himself he had been too hopeful. Still, perhaps he could steal a hat from a scarecrow or something. A hat would make a difference if he were only seen from a distance, and he had no intentions of getting too close to anyone.

He reached the dusty floor and decided it was time they went. The farmer couldn't possibly have had time to eat and would undoubtedly be back for his breakfast when he finished feeding his stock. They had to be away by then. He looked for Linda just as she looked up and gave a low, excited, shout.

'Larry, come here.'

He moved towards her. 'What is it, a top hat left over from Ascot?'

'No, something much more useful.' She stooped down and then came up to face him with lips moulded into an eager smile. 'Look at this.' In her hands she held a crutch.

He looked at it unimpressed. 'Well, it'd make a handy club I suppose. Why the excitement?'

'Idiot. Can't you see?'

'See what?'

'Oh, Larry,' she came towards him, smiling. 'See how much you need me. Here you have the perfect disguise and you can't even see it. You can't get rid of your bandages and injuries so the obvious thing to do is to add a few more on. You're going to have a gammy leg and your arm in a sling. All you'll get is sympathy. Why — we can even take a train up north. No one would expect you to do that. They'll expect you to act the way you meant to act, sneaking lifts aboard lorries and hiding during the day. And they'll expect you to be alone. This way, with me to help you, your chances are trebled.'

He stared into her flushed face and her excitement began to flood through him too. She was right again. The sheer audacity of it would carry him through. This way he could be almost there by nightfall, travelling the normal routes right under the noses of the police while they scoured the countryside for his hiding place. It would be a clever bluff, and all he needed was the courage to play it out.

He grabbed her suddenly and she let the crutch drop on his foot. For a second he held her and her startled eyes grew bright as she looked into his one excited eye. 'Nurse Denning, you're a genius,' he exclaimed.

'Linda,' she laughed. 'Call me Linda.'

'Linda you're a genius too.' He pulled her close and kissed her full on the mouth. The cherry ripe lips merged into his own and he felt a surge of desire flood through her as she strained closer in his arms. She was reaching up on her toes and he leaned back, lifting her with him as she clung around his neck. When he put her down her face was flushed and her eyes sparkling.

She said sternly, 'Be careful, you'll burst those stitches in your face.' And then she laughed.

Larry laughed with her although aware that it hurt his face, pulling at the stitches and almost bringing tears to his eyes. 'Come on,' he said. 'Let's get going.'

'Hold it a minute, you need a sling first. And get some of those newspapers out of that trunk. You can stuff your sock with them and make it look as though your foot is in plaster of paris.'

He nodded cheerfully and turned back towards the trunk while she slipped her hands beneath her skirt and wriggled her hips out of her half slip. When he turned she was just stepping out of the white silk.

'You were too quick,' she protested. She picked up the silk slip and began to rip off the lace frill around the bottom edge. 'You might look cute in a frilly sling,' she grinned. 'But it would hardly look genuine.' She tore the garment into a white square then folded it and slipped it into the pocket of her grey coat. 'Come on now. I'll decorate you up as soon as it becomes necessary. Right now let's get out of here before that farmer comes back.'

Larry nodded and picked up the crutch. Moving past her he peered through the cracks in the door to ensure that all was clear. The farmhouse showed no signs of life. The farmer's wife, if he had one, was obviously a later sleeper than her husband. Of the farmer or his dog there was nothing to be seen.

Cautiously Larry pushed open the barn door and stepped outside. After another swift glance around he nodded to Linda to join him. He pushed the barn door shut and together they ran through the trees towards the road. He held her arm as they fled, steering her through the copse and ducking beneath the branches. Close to the road, he pulled her to a halt, listening for any sounds of traffic or life. There were none and they went on to scramble over the low wire fence. Back on the road they paused for breath and then started briskly northwards away from the farm.

It was still only the first light of dawn and they walked for over an hour without seeing any more than a half dozen long distance lorries. When these passed Larry walked nearest to the grass verge with his bandaged face turned away, while Linda did her best to cover him. They covered two or three miles before reaching a small town, and here Linda made him stop while she arranged his disguise.

Removing his left shoe she padded his foot well with newspapers under his sock. Then she fixed the sling around his arm and stood back while he leaned on the crutch. She frowned.

'I think we're overdoing it. All that mass of white bandage rather hams it up a bit.' She came closer and removed the sling, then stepped back again. 'Yes, that's better. Just the crutch on its own should be all right.' She slipped the sling and his shoe into her overcoat pockets and smiled regretfully. 'I was a bit too hasty in tearing my clothes up, but I'll need them for bandages anyway when I do your face.'

He hopped towards her. 'You are the boss. Lead on.'

Using his crutch he followed her into the town. It was still early and the streets were deserted. A blue sign directed them to the station. A sleepy eyed official greeted them at the ticket window, his gaze straying curiously to Larry's face.

Larry forced himself to relax as Linda asked calmly, 'Can we get a direct train to Edinburgh from here?'

'You can miss, but it won't be for another hour. You're early.' The man's eyes were still on Larry.

Linda frowned. 'Give me two singles please. We'll wait for it.' Her frown turned to a wry smile. 'My brother has an appointment with a specialist at eleven-thirty, but our damned car broke down so we had to walk here.'

The ticket collector gave Larry another stare and then made a self-conscious start. He gave a quick smile. 'Sorry, Miss, but the train won't get you there that early. Still the doctor will probably see you in the circumstances.'

Linda treated him to another smile as she paid for the tickets. Watching her, Larry realized that here was another thing he needed her for. Without her, he had no money.

They moved on to the station and then into the waiting-room to pass away the next hour.

Larry said quietly, 'That story was good, but do you think he took it in?'

'I don't see why he shouldn't.' She smiled again. 'Just stop worrying.'

They talked on quietly as the next hour dragged past, until finally the northbound train steamed in. Larry tucked his crutch again under one arm and with his other about Linda's shoulders they boarded the train. Within a few minutes a whistle shrilled and they were on their way. Despite all his doubts it was as easy as that.

They sat back and relaxed as the train sped on, watching the rolling Yorkshire hills cruise past the windows. Soon Larry began to feel the reactions to his night's exertions setting in and without his realizing it his head lolled against Linda's shoulder. She smiled softly and let him doze.

When he awoke she was propping him back against a corner, she was already on her feet. The train was standing at a station. 'Go back to sleep,' she ordered him. 'I'm just slipping out to the bookstall. A map of northern Scotland will be a great help if I can get one.'

He nodded and closed his eyes obediently as she left him. He was dead tired and his brief sleep seemed to have left him wearier than before. He relaxed again, sinking inside himself and already half asleep. Unconsciousness began to wash over him and then abruptly a hand closed on his shoulder and shook

132

him awake. He sat up with a start.

It was Linda her eyes wide with alarm. 'Larry,' she blurted worriedly. 'Larry, look at this!' She thrust a folded paper into his hands and he read the headlines slowly.

PATIENT AND NURSE MISSING FROM MENTAL HOME
Police Hunt for Man with the Bandaged Face.

8

A Near Miss

The sudden shock jerked Larry out of his half dozing state with a start. He took the paper from her hand and read it through slowly. It took some time for the facts to sink in.

The paper carried the story of his breakout from the nursing home and a statement to the effect that they were now certain that he was the last man out of the McArnot mine. There was a big sketch of how he looked with his face covered in the white shroud of bandages, rather like the head of a mummy with one glaring eye. 'Also missing from the hospital,' the report continued, 'is 21-year-old Nurse Linda Denning. Mrs. A. N. Whitwell, a bedridden widow living in a cottage near the home, stated today that late last night she saw a man with a white bandaged head carrying an apparently unconscious girl in his arms. Having no telephone and being unable to leave her bed there was nothing Mrs. Whitwell could do until a neighbour called this morning. The police say they are anxious to interview the man with the bandaged head who gives his name as Larry Brown.'

Linda said slowly, 'They think that you have kidnapped me, Larry. They don't realize.'

He lifted his head slowly. 'Well, I'm wanted by the police all right. They think I'm a dangerous killer.'

She looked down at the headlines again. 'So soon though. I thought we had until the evening papers came out at least.'

Larry studied the top of the paper. 'Late edition. They sure didn't waste time getting to the number one spot though. Some newshawk's idea of a scoop, rushing in before the evenings come out.' He scowled as best he could in his bandages. 'Hell, they must have been on to it early though. I counted on much longer than this.'

She managed a short laugh. 'Well,

maybe it's later than you think. You've slept all morning, it's now well past twelve.'

He sat upright as the train began to move again. He hadn't been aware that he had slept so long. 'Where are we?' he asked.

'We're through Newcastle, just about half way I should think.' She sat down beside him and they studied the paper together. Really the report was fairly brief, mostly taken up by the headlines and the old lady's story. They re-read it through and then Linda ventured grimly, 'It looks bad doesn't it?'

'It sure does. It's hinted pretty plainly that I'm a killer, which means they must think I murdered those men in the mine. They also think I've kidnapped you.'

'Well, we can prove them wrong about that any time. That's just a mistake.'

'And the other?'

She smiled and squeezed his arm. 'They're wrong about that too Larry, and when we find out what did happen down that mine we'll prove that to them as well. Don't worry about it. We knew it would hit the headlines sooner or later. What difference does it make to us that one editor has stolen a three or four hour march on the evening papers.' She was trying to boost his moral now and went on. 'And as for that bit about me, that might be a help. They gave no description and they'll expect you to be hiding somewhere with me as a hostage. Not travelling openly while I pose as your sister. Our chances are still good.'

He said quietly, 'Now that they know you're with me they'll print your description too when the evening papers come out. If we stick together they'll be bound to get us.'

'Not the way we're going about it. Now that they think you're holding me hostage they have all the more reason to expect you to stay in hiding. They'd never think of looking for us in the open now. Our only risk is that someone may suspect us by chance, and if we act natural they'll probably figure that their imagination is running riot and forget us.'

There was something in what she

said and Larry's confidence began to climb. He remembered his password and thought suddenly: It was a damned good game to win. There was more of a challenge to it than ever before. And the chances of pulling off a bluff were equally good.

He said suddenly, 'Maybe you're right, Linda. I hope so because I've still got to go on. It's the only way for me.'

She smiled. 'That's the way. Now let me rearrange those bandages before we reach the next station and someone gets in here. If I can fix it so that you can see with both eyes it might help. They're looking for a kind of one-eyed monster.'

He sat still while she began to unwind the bandages, watching her slim fingers move about his face. She unwound enough to be able to see his wounds and made him wince when she pulled the remainder back. She said thoughtfully. 'They're as good as can be expected. It won't be long before the last of those stitches can come out. Considering that this is only the fifth day they've been in you're healing remarkably fast.'

He grinned. It no longer hurt him to smile or talk now. 'That's the result of good nursing. The best in fact.'

'Flatterer.' She studied the closed gash above his right eye with an intent expression. 'I think I can do it.' She began to replace the bandages, this time leaving both eyes clear but coming down lower over his brows. Her hands were sure and swift and when she had finished the bandages no longer obstructed his vision in any way. Except for when he tried to look at the ceiling without lifting his head.

She eyed the results and said cheerfully, 'Well at least you're no longer likely to terrify any old ladies or small dogs you happen to meet. You don't look half so menacing as you did with one eye.'

He said abruptly, 'Why are you doing this, helping me I mean?'

Her gaze became hesitant. 'I don't know really. Maybe it's because I'm the only one who doesn't believe you're guilty. Maybe it's because I don't like the unfair way the odds are stacked against you. And maybe it's just because I like you. I honestly don't really know.'

He waited in silence for her to go on but she had no more to say. She was staring vaguely out of the window.

He said slowly, 'Do you know what was the greatest thing you ever did for me?'

She looked back, and shook her head.

'You gave me a name. Until then I was just an unknown tramp they'd picked out of the gutter. Just a nobody, but you gave me a name. Howell was content to call me young man, and the police just called me sir, but you gave me a name. I think that was when I began to — '

He stopped there, suddenly startled by what he had been about to say. He had nearly said, to love you. But he couldn't say that, even if he could be sure it was true. He couldn't say that until he had penetrated the depths of that old mine and found out the truth about himself. Not until then, and perhaps not even then.

Perhaps she guessed what he had been about to say, but she gave no sign. She leaned her head on his shoulder and dozed as the train roared northwards.

★ ★ ★

Their journey took another three hours and when they finally pulled into Edinburgh station their positions had been reversed. Linda had awakened while Larry had succumbed to the jogging of the train and slept. She gave him a shake as the train stopped, and the sudden jolt brought him awake.

'Come on, brother,' she said cheerfully. 'You've got an appointment at the hospital remember.'

He stared at her dazedly and then realized abruptly that they were no longer alone. While he slept other passengers had boarded the train. There were three of them, two men and a woman.

'Your sister's been telling us about your accident,' one of the men told him seriously. 'I sure hope that doctor fixes you up all right. It must be terrible to be trapped in a burning car.'

'Yes,' Larry agreed hopefully. 'It was.'

He felt his heart pounding over-fast as the three struggled out into the corridor with their bags.

'Need a hand?' asked the woman sympathetically.

'No thanks,' Linda gave her a smile. 'We've no luggage so we can manage all right. We'll just give the platform time to clear a bit.'

Larry waited until the corridor outside was empty and then breathed a sigh of relief.

'That shook me,' he said slowly. 'I think it's about time you told me what our story is in case it happens again. I'd better be able to back you up if necessary.'

She grinned. 'It's a simple story. You were driving your car when a lorry crashed into you. The car went up in flames and your face was badly burnt before you were pulled out. Your ankle got broken too. At the moment we're on our way to see a skin specialist about your face. When we get on the train to Inverness we'll be going back. Our story then is that our home is Inverness.'

'Why Inverness?'

'Because from there we can hire a car to take us the rest of the way. We could go a little further by train but it would mean getting off at some small station where we would be sure to arouse suspicion. We won't in a large town like Inverness.'

'Fair enough.' He looked out at the now almost deserted platform. 'Come on, let's move.'

They left the train and made their way through the barrier. The ticket collector nodded them on without a second glance as he took their tickets. Larry breathed a sigh of relief and received a smile from Linda as she led the way to the buffet. She ordered tea and sandwiches and then left him to eat them at a corner table while she went out to get the tickets for the next stage of their journey. He felt slightly uneasy as she vanished though the door.

After a few minutes he began to sip the sweet tea when a sudden commotion at the door made him look up. He watched half a dozen railway workers push their way in. They made for the counter and spent a couple of minutes teasing the waitress as she drained tea from the large silver urn. Then they came over and seated themselves at the table next to Larry, one of them pulled out an evening paper.

Larry stiffened as he watched the man read the headlines. He could see quite clearly the one-eyed mummy picture of himself on the front page.

The tea turned sour in Larry's mouth and he had difficulty in swallowing it. It was true that ninety-nine out of every hundred people who read that story would pass it by without a second thought. But there was always that hundredth one. He listened as the railway worker began to discuss the story with his friends, feeling glaringly conspicuous in his corner.

It was obvious what the railway man thought. In a broad Scots accent he was giving his exact opinion on what should happen to a 'murdering swine who could harm a poor wee lassie that's done naething but nurse him.' He had very definite views on the matter.

The tea in Larry's hand grew cold as he listened. The sudden vacuum in his stomach grew even colder. The railwayman was gesturing with his hands as his eyes roved around his friends at his table, and then abruptly his eyes fell on Larry.

The man was startled, his eyes wide with sudden fear as he saw the white face. Larry knew instantly that there was no doubt in the other's mind. The man knew exactly who he was.

For tense seconds they held each other's eyes then Larry turned away, his brain racing frantically. His crutch was against the wall out of reach and his stuffed out foot hidden beneath the table. Without them he was stripped of his disguise. To run would mean that the hunt would be up within seconds and with his white face he would never get out of the station. If he stayed the porter was going to start yelling for a policeman any minute. His only chance was to allay the man's suspicions.

He acted on impulse. Before the porter could get his speech back he asked quickly, 'Can one of you gentlemen do me a favour? My sister left my crutch out of reach; if you could just pass it — '

The whole table glanced round. A dozen eyes studied his white face, and then:

'Certainly, sir.' The nearest man to him got up and slowly handed him the crutch.

'Thank you.' Larry was surprised at the calm way his voice was sounding, judging by the way his inside was reacting it should have been twisted and stammering. He got up slowly balancing on one leg as he tucked the crutch under his arm. Calmly, without hurry, he shuffled up to the counter.

There was no queue and the woman by the tea urn gave him a nervous look as he came up. 'Another tea, please,' he said quietly. He began to feel in his pockets for a coin.

Another fear hit him then. He was wearing stolen clothes, he had no money. To be unable to pay was going to create more unwanted attention. He felt trapped, snared in the coils of circumstance. If only he had a coin he might yet bluff his way. His hands went frantically through all the pockets of his clothing, through his jacket and trousers. There was no money. The woman behind the counter pushed the cup of tea towards him and waited expectantly.

His mouth was dry, there was no moisture in his throat at all. The only moisture was the sweat on his forehead. He forced a smile.

'I — I'm sorry, I don't seem to have any money. I thought I had but — but I must have lost it. Will it be all right if my sister pays for this when she comes back.'

'Your sister?' There was no encouragement in the woman's tone.

'Yes, the young lady who was with me. We were sitting over there.' He gestured vaguely to the corner. 'She just went out to get the tickets.' He forced another smile. 'I must be getting too dependent on her. This will teach me not to rely on her for so much. Only a fool would come out with no money in his pockets.'

The woman smiled suddenly. 'All right,

sir, I'm not supposed to but I'll trust you until your sister gets back.'

'Thank you. This makes me feel such a fool.' Relief was washing over him as he picked the cup up. 'Thanks again,' he smiled apologetically and limped back towards his seat.

The railwaymen watched him sit down and then the one who had retrieved his crutch said cheerfully, 'You should have said it was just a cup of tea ye needed. I'd have fetched it for ye, sir.'

'Oh, that's all right.' He had to force a smile again. 'It's not so hard to put up with when you can do a few things for yourself. Besides, a little exercise keeps the rest of me fit.'

'Ah ken what ye mean, sir,' a thin man on the far side of the table spoke up. 'Mah brother broke his leg once and resented evra thing we did for'm. Said it made him feel helpless to sit and be fussed over.'

'That's the way I feel. It's only a broken ankle I keep telling them, but they will act as though I can't move an inch.'

'You're on your way to the hospital then?' It was the man with the paper speaking, still suspicious.

'No, on our way back. I've just had to visit the skin specialist.' He touched his face gently. 'I lost a lot of skin off my face in the accident. My car crashed and caught fire. It was burns mostly.'

'That's a rough bit of luck.' It was the helpful one again. He sipped his tea and added, 'Motor-cars are damned dangerous things.'

Larry laughed. 'Don't I know it.' He drank half the tea he had brought, feeling their eyes still on him. When he put the cup down he saw the thin man glancing at his friend's paper on the table. He looked up and grinned.

'Ye'll have to be careful, sir. They'll be mistaking you for this laddie.'

Larry laughed again, despite the way his stomach squirmed inside. 'I'm getting used to it,' he said. 'Twice this morning I've had people call the police over to me. That last time I had to wait for my sister to come out of a shop and clear me. That fellow's a damned nuisance.'

The suspicious one looked disappointed. 'Ay, I suppose it is an awkward coincidence for ye. Nae doot they'll pick him up before long though.'

Larry nodded, his nerves were really taut now and he wondered how much longer he could bluff his way along. If only Linda would come back. He realized then that she had been gone some time, it was almost half past three. Over twenty minutes. What could be keeping her for so long?

He said as easily as he could, 'By nightfall we should be back in Inverness anyway. After that I shall keep near home where I'm known. It's only strangers that get suspicious.'

'You live in Inverness then? You don't speak like a Scot?'

He nodded. 'We've been living there for several months now. Long enough to feel at home but not long enough to learn the accent.' He wondered again what was keeping Linda, he had almost forgotten his own dangers in the worry for her.

The owner of the paper said suddenly, 'You say you're with your sister. Where is she now then?' He was still doubtful.

'I don't know, I wish I did.' For once he could answer wholeheartedly. 'She went out to get the tickets.' He looked up towards the clock on the wall and felt cold. She had been gone half an hour, much longer than was necessary. He began to visualize all the things that might have happened and realized how utterly lost he was without her. He needed Linda Denning much more than he previously knew.

Then the suspicious one said quietly, 'You ken, I still canna get over how similar ye look tae this laddie in the paper. If only he hadna the other eye covered.'

Larry felt as though the other had a stranglehold on his throat. The remark took him by surprise and he couldn't think of an answer. The man was watching him closely and he felt his throat working uselessly. All this talk and he was still trapped.

Then Linda Denning said brightly, 'Hullo, Larry. Have you left me any sandwiches?'

151

He looked up to find her standing beside him, smiling.

For a moment he was unable to speak and then he forced down all the questions he wanted to ask her. Turning to the railwaymen he said slowly, 'This is my sister, Anne.' He had almost said Linda but her name was in the newspaper.

She smiled. 'Well I'm glad to see you found some company. But right now we've got a train to catch. It leaves at three forty-five.'

Larry glanced at the suspicious porter and saw complete disappointment written in his eyes. The man accepted the appearance of the sister whose existence he had doubted as proof that he was wrong. The mystery killer would be travelling alone. Not openly with a woman. The girl who might be with him would be his prisoner and not his helper. Besides he would never be fool enough to come into Edinburgh station. The man's mind was an open book and Larry had to fight down a laugh as he read it.

He said good-bye to his unwanted

friends and then waited while Linda paid for the cup of tea he had had. Her share of the sandwiches she slipped in her pocket to eat on the train before helping him outside.

When the door closed behind them he heaved a sigh of relief. 'That was a near miss. Where the devil have you been?'

'Pawning my ring,' she said simply. 'We had half an hour to wait and we were short of money. So when I bought the tickets and found we were nearly broke I went out and found a pawn shop.'

'You shouldn't — ' he began, but she cut him off.

'Later Larry. At the moment we've got another problem.'

'What's that?'

'The police.' Her voice was taut and nervous. 'There's a lot of uniformed police moving about now, and there's another man in plain clothes leaning against the barrier to the train. I'm pretty sure he's a policeman too.'

9

The Road North

Larry stopped dead in the middle of the station, oblivious of the rush of people hurrying to their trains. The noise and bustle of the busy terminus was suddenly lost to him as he faltered slowly, 'That can't be, Linda. The police can't possibly know that we're here.'

'Of course not. But they are keeping watch just in case. I think they must be watching all routes north. They know you've lost your memory and must be expecting you to make for the only place you know that has a link with your past. The McArnot mine. They're just covering every approach you might try to use.'

He grimaced. 'Then we're finished. Our one hope was that we could bluff our way through because they'd never think to watch the open routes. Now

154

they're on the lookout we'll never get aboard that train.'

She said softly, 'We can try, Larry. Keep up the cripple act and go on. If we keep it natural there's still a fifty fifty chance we'll get through. They're on the lookout for a man alone. A man with no bandages but a scarred face. I read a newspaper outside that said you were certain to have dumped me and stripped off the bandages. This way we can still bluff our way through.'

'But he'll suspect. He must suspect.'

'Of course he will. The first thing he'll think of is that you're the hunted man. Then he'll doubt. He just won't believe that you'd be crazy enough to walk right through that barrier. And it's fifty fifty that we'll get away with it.'

'All right,' he conceded. 'I'll take even odds.' He swallowed the fear that was in his throat and together they approached the barrier.

The plain clothes man beside the ticket collector had policeman written all over him. A man with nothing to fear would never notice but to a fugitive from the law the signs were glaringly obvious. The detective leaned against the barrier with both hands in his pockets. His alert eyes roaming the faces of the crowd. He had to watch them. That was his job there. And it was that that marked him for certain. He let his gaze rove the station, scrutinizing every face that passed through the barrier. Then he saw Larry and suspicion crossed his face.

Linda murmured, 'Be bold, Larry.' And then aloud. 'How does your face feel now?'

'Sore, but getting easier. I don't think that damned doctor tried to be gentle.'

She laughed as she handed their tickets over for clipping. 'Don't worry, darling. It's over for another fortnight. You ought to think yourself lucky really. Those burns could have blinded you.'

'You try feeling lucky with half your face burnt away.'

She paused to replaced the clipped tickets in her purse. 'Come on. Another few hours and you'll be home with your feet up.' She helped him through the barrier and they limped slowly down the platform. Larry couldn't say another word, his throat had seized up completely. He wanted to look back, desperately wanted to look back, but didn't dare.

Behind them the detective watched them go. He took one hand out of his pocket and rubbed his nose. It wasn't possible. The man he was after just couldn't be such a fool as to keep those bandages on. He watched their retreating backs and thought suddenly. If they look back. If the man looked back he would follow them. He watched them board the waiting train but neither looked back. He turned away then. He had been told to look out for a lone man with a badly scarred face, and that man just might slip through while he was gawking after the cripple. The inspector would never forgive him for that. He saw the ticket collector watching him with expectant eyes and laughed.

'Nay mon, the laddie we're after'll be alone. And it's tae much to hope that he'll just walk into *my* hands like tha'.'

The ticket collector laughed with him

and carried on clipping tickets.

Aboard the train both Larry and Linda were sweating. It was a long time before Linda could smile.

'Well, we made it, Larry — and he didn't ask a single question.'

Larry said slowly, 'He just didn't know what to think. He must have been afraid of making a fool of himself if he stopped us. I shan't be sorry to get out of here though. I'm still not sure whether I convinced those railway workers.'

She sat down beside him. 'What happened there?'

He told her as the train moved out. While they talked an elderly man with his wife and three children joined them, and after that their conversation was limited. Their unwanted companions vanished behind copies of the *Football News* and *Woman's Own* respectively. The three small boys studied them with interest until their mother snapped at them in a flustered Scots burr for staring. She apologized awkwardly.

Linda waved the apologies aside. 'He's getting used to stares since his accident,' she told the woman cheerily. 'All children are alike.'

They finished the sandwiches they had bought at the buffet and then stared out of the windows uncomfortably. Neither of their adult companions showed any interest in them, setting examples for the children no doubt. They sat in silence and were grateful when the whole family got up at Queensferry and went out.

The train nosed out over the Forth Bridge and they watched the lattice work of brown steel flash by. Far below the waters of the firth looked dull and angry, moving sluggishly in low waves. Sea birds screamed and wheeled in the greying sky and then the criss-cross walls of steel and the glint of the sea were behind them. The train roared on ever northwards.

For a while they were able to talk again, and spread out the map Linda had bought previously to plan their route. They found Shieldonnel, the nearest village to the mine, a few miles to the north of Loch Broom on the sea coast. They plotted their course from Inverness along the main A835, they had between fifty and sixty miles to drive once they left the train.

They folded the map and settled down for the rest of the journey. Then at the next station another trio of passengers climbed in, and this time they were much more talkative. A thin scraggy man, the sort who was in love with the sound of his own voice, did most of it. He rambled on and they listened attentively. Once they had offered the brother and sister routine and mentioned the non-existent car crash and hospital, they were content to say nothing. They let the others do the conversing and restricted themselves to agreeing whenever it seemed unlikely to start an argument.

For over four hours they had to listen to the chatter of their companions. Four long dragged out hours. They tired of the scenery long before they reached Inverness. Linda leaned against Larry with his arm close about her shoulders. Her weight pinned his arm to the semi-soft back of the seat and after a while it began to ache. It was his left arm, the bandaged one, and he realized it was the first time he had given it a thought since breaking out. In time the continued weight made it throb but she was half asleep and he ignored it.

After a time he fell asleep himself and when he woke the train was slowing to a stop at Inverness. He woke Linda and together they went out to again run the gauntlet of the police.

However this time there was no lounging plainclothes man at the barrier. They went through without a hitch.

Linda said triumphantly, 'We must be through the cordon. They must think that you can't possibly be this far north.'

Larry limped along beside her into the street. 'Let's hope they keep on thinking it.'

They moved on into the town until they found a garage that offered cars for hire. Here Linda left him in the shadows of a shop doorway while she went across to make inquiries. After ten minutes that dragged interminably she finally drove out of the garage at the wheel of a grey Consul. She drew up beside him and he swung into the seat next to her. Instantly she let the clutch in and drove away.

She glanced over at him and her face was pale. 'Hell,' she breathed fervently. 'That made me sweat. I gave him my licence and insurance to check and then it dawned on me that he might easily know my name from the newspapers. I never thought of that before I went in, or I wouldn't have tried it.'

'What did he say?' Larry was tense.

'Nothing,' she laughed tightly and shifted the car into top gear. 'He didn't seem to notice anything wrong. He asked me if there was anyone in Inverness who could vouch or me before he left the car go. I gave him a fake address and he seemed quite satisfied. He just took my word and wrote it down.'

'Then we'd better get out of here before he checks.'

'I don't think he will. He didn't seem at all suspicious. I didn't know I was such a convincing liar. I remembered the name of one of the streets we passed and gave him an address there. It came out quite pat. It was a nasty few minutes though.'

She gave him a drawn smile as she swung the car north at a roundabout and headed out of town on the A9 to the west.

They left Inverness and for a while drove with the dark, menacing waters of Beauly Firth on their right. Larry's cripple disguise would be of no more use to him now, and while Linda drove he discarded the newspapers that had padded his sock and replaced his shoe. They drove in silence until they had wound through the town of Beauty and turned north. Then Linda stopped at an open village café and slipped out to buy sandwiches and lemonade. For by now they were ravenously hungry.

When she returned Larry had moved over behind the wheel. He said quietly, 'I'll drive. Did you have any trouble?'

'Well, yes and no.' She climbed into the car and settled back as he drove off. 'Nobody seemed to suspect, but I was warned not to pick up any hitch hikers. The whole of Scotland seems to be on the lookout for you. The police seem to be sure that you'll head this way.'

Larry's hands tightened on the wheel.

'That settles it then.'

'Settles what?'

'I'm dropping you off, Linda.' He glanced down at her surprised face. 'At the very next town.'

'Why this sudden desire to get rid of me?'

'It's not that. You know that. But from here on we might get caught at any time. Your presence won't help me and will only incriminate you. I don't want you to get into any trouble, Linda. You've taken enough risks.'

She smiled. 'I'm not leaving you at this stage, Larry, and I think you know it. Anyway — thanks for the thought.'

'Linda, be sensible.'

'I am being sensible, Larry. You see I'm already incriminated. I can't just suddenly turn up in Scotland and tell the police it was all a mistake. I've got too much to explain.'

'We could make up some kind of story. How I forced you, and how you finally escaped.'

'They'd punch holes through it, Larry. They'll know it wasn't possible for you

164

to force me all this way. An unmarked man with a gun in his pocket might have done it, but not you. You're unarmed, and then there's your face. The police are looking for a man with a bandaged face holding a helpless girl. Any girl with spirit would only have to attract attention to get you caught. And it's impossible to travel from Lincolnshire to here without getting a chance to do that.' She laughed softly. 'No, Larry, once the police discover that I'm still alive, I'm going to have a lot of questions to answer. So I might as well stick with you.'

'They — they think you're dead then?'

'Well, the way they put it they don't hold much hope for me which means the same thing. I read it in the headlines of a late paper lying on the counter in that café.'

'And they're on the lookout for me all around here, isn't that what you were told?'

'That's right. The police must have reasoned that you'd murder me and then make for the mine alone. They know it's the only link you have with your past. Even though they're convinced that you must have shot those three men in the mine they still don't doubt that the horror of it drove it from your mind. I knew that back at the nursing home.' She passed her tongue over her lips and said slowly, 'You know, Larry, going to that mine is like putting your head into a tiger's jaws. They must be waiting for you.'

'I've got no choice. I suppose I could turn back and run, but then I'd always be running and never know the truth. So, I've really got no choice.'

She placed her hand on his shoulder. 'I know, and I've got no choice either. If I let you drop me off like you want to, I should never forgive myself for letting you down. You see you still need me, Larry, if only as a friend to boost your morale. Everyone needs a friend.'

He moved his right hand from the wheel and covered hers as it rested on his shoulder. Her eyes still had that soft quality of warmth, even in the semi-darkness.

He said quietly, 'Okay, Linda, we'll stay as a team. You and I against the rest. All the way.'

She laughed and they drove on through the black shadows of the night, the broad beam of the headlights cutting a wide lane through the darkness. They followed the road north until they turned off at Dingwall and headed west on the A834. Larry pushed his toe down on the accelerator and the miles flashed beneath them. Speed possessed him now. He was on the last lap and in no mood to dawdle.

For over an hour they raced through the blackness, Larry crouching like a white faced ghost at the wheel. Had anyone seen him bearing down on them through the night another legend might have been born in the lonely highlands. A legend of a ghoul-driver who drove a grey car with the skill of a maniac. For the pale glow from the dashlight gave a sinister aspect to his mummified features.

They reached Loch Broom, its surface black and stirred with ruffled movement.

The road followed the north shore and they drove into a cutting wind that swept in from the North Atlantic. The air tasted salty now and as they neared the sea-mouth of the loch they heard the faint growl of the breakers on the rugged coastline.

They turned north at the sea-mouth, feeling the stiff wind howl against their car. The night was black as pitch, no moon and only occasion glimmers of light from the houses and villages along the roadside. The only sound was the sound of the sea.

And then, a bare half-dozen miles short of their objective, a car suddenly appeared in the headlights. A large black car, stationary and blocking the road. A figure in a black uniform stepped forwards and raised his hand in a signal to halt. Two more men moved behind him. They were police.

Larry swore bitterly. It was a road block.

10

Burglary

Larry braked instinctively, stabbing his foot down viciously in a way that made the car screech and flung him sharply forward against the wheel. Then angry determination killed all thoughts of caution and he hit the accelerator instead. The headlights showed a gap to the right of the parked car, a wide verge that just might be wide enough to allow him a passage through. He wrenched the wheel round and sent the car rocketing towards it.

The jolt as they hit the verge almost tore the wheel from his hands and threw Linda sprawling down the seat on top of him. The rear wheels mounted the grass and the car bucked wildly. The wheel hit Larry across the chest and then his weight was jerked back with an agonizing pull against the bandages on his left arm.

169

Linda yelled with alarm and outside the three policemen scattered in confusion. A peaked cap rolled in the road and one man fell crashing on his face.

The car bounced savagely over the grass and Larry aimed it clumsily at the space between the back of the police car and the low stone wall that bordered the road beyond the verge. The gap was far too small but it was too late to brake now. Their bonnet crashed through, smashing into the police car in a glancing blow that sent it skidding out of their path. The harsh rending of metal told him that they had half torn their fender off and then the rear of the car crashed against the wall. Larry wrenched the wheel back towards the road and put his foot hard down. The car leapt forward, bouncing erratically over the grass before it hit the level road again. And then they were away, leaving the road block behind them.

Larry glanced back to see the three blue uniforms piling hurriedly into their own car. They were lightning fast and barely a minute elapsed before they had straightened their vehicle and were racing in pursuit. By then Larry had quite a start and the lights of the police car were almost a quarter of a mile behind him.

He kept his foot down and glanced across at Linda. She was sitting up slowly her face pale and trembling. Somehow she managed to find a smile. A tight smile but a smile.

'Larry don't ever do that again without warning.' Her voice was surprisingly calm. 'You'll give me heart attack, or pink kittens or something.'

He grinned, relieved that she was all right. 'Sorry, Linda, it was just impulse. There wasn't time for warnings. I even scared myself.'

He had to slow down for a bend and she glanced back through the rear window. 'They're gaining, Larry. They're gaining fast.'

He put his foot down again, screeching and skidding around the curves of the road. The speedometer reached sixty-five and in the darkness he dared not go faster. Behind them the police car slowly but surely closed the gap.

Linda said tensely, 'We'll never outrun them, Larry. They've got a faster car and they know the roads.'

He glanced in his driving mirror and saw the dazzle of the pursuing car's lights coming ever nearer. He pressed his foot harder and saw the needle climb to seventy. It was suicidal and useless. The car behind still gained.

Linda hung on to her seat as the car screamed around the sudden bends. It only needed one really sharp bend and they would never make it. She began to sweat, every second visualizing the tearing impact as they shot off the road and the car overturned in a mass of flame. Larry's bound face showed no expression of his feelings. His eyes glared straight ahead.

'How close?' he said suddenly.

She fought for balance as he skidded the car into a bend then glanced back. 'About two hundred yards — and gaining.'

'Damn them,' he said viciously, and slightly slackened his foot on the accelerator.

She saw the speedometer needle drop a fraction and asked quickly, 'What are you going to do?'

'Run them off the road. It's our only chance.'

She didn't ask how, she merely swallowed dryly and waited.

He said slowly, 'I can only pray that if it comes off I don't kill any of them. But it's our chance. We'll never shake them off.'

She nodded without speaking, hanging on, white and tensed as he drove the car on at reduced but still suicide speed.

He watched the lights of the police car creep up in the driving mirror and felt the tension building up in his chest. His stomach was a-flutter and his hands slippery on the wheel. He almost crashed the car into the verge through watching the mirror instead of the road.

He said hoarsely, 'How far?'

'About eighty yards.' Her voice was cracked.

He swung the car screeching into another slow curve. He had to let them get closer than that. Closer but not too close. They had to be at the right distance.

He asked again, 'How far?'

'They're closing, about seventy.'

Seventy! Seventy yards. Still too far. About forty would be right. He had to wait.

She said tightly, 'Sixty.'

A pause.

'Fifty.'

'They're closing fast, forty.'

Savagely Larry hit the brake, jamming his foot down with all his strength. The car screamed and the wheels locked. The steering wheel almost jerked out of his hand.

The driver of the police car saw the stoplights of the Consul flash a fierce and angry red. Instinctively he hit his own brakes but he was already seconds behind. The grey Consul was slap in the middle of the road and there was only one way of avoiding a crash. He took it. He wrenched the wheel of the skidding car and careered up the side of the road, missing the back of the Consul by the width of a matchbox.

The bonnet of the police car crashed through a low stone wall and the driver braced his arms desperately. Somehow he kept the car straight, racing across the moorland until it eventually came to rest with the front axle bogged down in a shallow ditch. The engine stalled and all three occupants swore in unison.

Larry hit the accelerator the moment he heard the police car crash through the wall. He raced away while Linda hung on grimly. After a mile he slackened speed and stopped. He switched his lights off and waited.

There was no sign of pursuit.

He looked at Linda slowly, her coat had fallen open and her breasts moved tremulously beneath the red blouse.

'What happened to them?' he asked.

'They ran off the road,' she managed weakly. 'It's all right though, they didn't turn over. They stayed upright and shot across the field. I don't think they could have been hurt. At least not seriously.'

'Thank God,' he said, and meant it. He started the car again and moved off slowly with only the side-lights to guide him. He said grimly. 'We'll have to ditch the car somewhere now. We passed the turning to Shieldonnel Cove a couple of miles back and it's no use turning round. We'll make our way to the coast on foot.' He swore angrily. 'Hell, who would have expected a road block back there?'

'We might have done,' she pointed out, her voice more even now that she had had time to recover. 'Anyone coming this way by car would have to use that road. It's the only one. Roads are pretty few this far up in the highlands and the nearest alternative is to circle right up north and then come down again.'

He shrugged. 'I guess so. We might have guessed they'd keep an eye on that one road. And now they'll be on the alert. Those men at the road block must have recognized my face at the wheel.'

She frowned and murmured quietly, 'They'll search the moors and mountains once they realize we've ditched the car, but we'll still have a few hours before they get properly organized. We can reach the mine in that time.'

Larry nodded grimly and drove on.

He kept his speed low and after a while found a rough track leading off the road. He turned off there and hid the car behind a hay-stack further up.

'From here I'm afraid we walk it,' he said.

They hurried back to the road on foot, crossed it and climbed over the low stone wall on the other side. The ground rose steeply here and they branched off away from the road in a tangent to the southwest. An angle that should bring them out on the coast near Shieldonnel and the mine. It was damp and cold. The wind howled through unseen mountain crags and the mist swallowed them up. They left the road behind and below them, lost in the black night.

The rough ground made them stumble from time to time as they picked their way around rocks and hillocks. Their feet caught in the long grass and the close roots of heather. The vague shapes of mossy boulders and stumpy bushes and trees kept looming up before them and made Linda shiver. Like lost souls they made their way across the flank of the mountainside; the man an eerie, frightening, figure in the mist with his white bound face, and the girl stumbling valiantly at his side.

They came to a saddle-backed ridge and the ground levelled off for a few much needed yards. Black hills rose on either side and then the ground sloped down again. The earth became marshy as they entered a low hollow and their feet squelched in the wet grass. Neither spoke, for they had no breath to waste. Many times only Larry's arm about Linda's shoulders kept the girl from falling when she tripped.

The mist thinned a little and on their left they could make out the rugged heights of the mountain rising black and solid against the dark clouds. Ahead the ground rose in another steep incline. The wind was cutting through the hollow with a quivering moan, ripping through them as though they were naked.

Larry glanced down at Linda. She was watching the path ahead, picking her way grimly. Her mouth was set and her dark curls flapping in the wind, were already damp from the mist. He wished then that he had forced her to remain behind, but he knew she would never have consented. Bitterly he pushed on.

For nearly an hour they walked though the thick swirling night. Following the slope of the mountain, or veering into heather flanked glens. Always maintaining their approximate south-west course. They picked their way around some thickets of gorse, wary of the sharp thorns, then abruptly they almost walked into a shallow stream that spilled down the centre of the glen.

Linda hesitated and Larry swung one arm under her knees and lifted her up.

'No point in us both getting wet,' he said grinning. He tried to stop his teeth chattering as he said it.

He stepped out into the stream and ice-cold water swirled about his ankles and rose to his knees. Smooth pebbles shifted under his feet and he almost fell. The water rushed around his thighs and he held the girl high on his chest. The cold made him grit his teeth and he almost ran the last few paces to the far bank. He kept going and smiled down at the girl in his arms. She snuggled against his chest for a moment and then reluctantly ordered him to set her down. Even more reluctantly he obeyed.

They faced another stiff climb as the hills closed in on them, until finally a rugged mass of grass-grown rock blocked their path. Wearily Larry started up it, scrambling for footholds and pulling Linda up behind him. Once she lost her footing and he drew her up bodily with one arm. The effort sapped the bulk of his energy and when he reached the top he was breathing heavily. Linda too was panting, her hair dishevelled and her bosom rising.

They started walking again without a word. The sea wind was fierce and bitter here, beating their faces and ruffling their clothes. They were both tired now and both shivering with cold. Not even the strain and exertion of climbing and walking had been able to keep them warm in the damp mist. Larry felt his legs weakening and decided that soon they would have to take a rest. But the cold made him reluctant to stop and when Linda assured him that she was quite fit enough to keep going he changed his mind. They might be cold walking but if they stopped they might even freeze.

The slope levelled out at last and then started to descend. A slippery descent covered in loose, sliding shale. They found themselves slithering down too fast, unable to stop.
Linda uttered a little yell of alarm as they shot down hand in hand. Larry used his free hand to grab at the surface of the slide but without effect. Then the descent ended in a deep hollow and they fell over and rolled down into it. Larry finished up underneath with Linda sprawling across his chest. Fortunately the hollow was dry.

Linda pushed herself to her knees and uttered an indignant, 'Oh!' The tone told Larry she was more startled than hurt and he raised himself on one elbow and chuckled. She was surveying her ruined stockings with a look of distaste.

'It's not funny,' she snapped. And laughed.

They sat up together and got their breath back, both relieved that neither had been hurt. Above them the shale slope ran upwards at a sharp angle. Small rocks and stones rattled down on them from the disrupted trail marked by their fall and they hastily moved to the other side of the hollow. They were well under wind here and by mutual consent they rested. Waiting for the heave of their breathing to steady up again.

After a while they felt the cold begin to seep into them from the damp earth and moved off out of the far side of the hollow. They were slightly rested now and made better headway. The mist was still too close for them to see much of their surroundings and they had to feel their way down into another low glen and climb yet another slope. Another descent left them breathless and Larry realized that coming down took more energy than going up. Coming down they couldn't help moving fast, unable to check themselves. Going up they could at least set their own pace.

Then abruptly they came out on the brow of a hill and the wind was savage in their faces. From ahead they heard the wild anger of the sea as it beat on the rocky coastline. The air was wet with a tang of salt to it and they knew that somewhere below, and not far ahead, the land ended in a barrier of sea-washed rock. Turning to their right they could just make out a few indications of light, almost hidden in the mist, that could only be Shieldonnel cove.

Linda said breathlessly, 'That must be Shieldonnel to our right. Which way is the mine?'

'It's to the south of the village, which means it must be on our left somewhere. We'd better follow the coastline along.' He almost had to shout to make himself heard above the wind.

He wound his arm around her waist and led her along the brow of the hill towards the south. The sound of the sea breaking joined with the howl of the wind to assault their ears. Larry's legs were almost frozen with cold from his wade through the stream and he began to shiver as they went. Linda was trembling with cold despite the overcoat that the wind whipped noisily around her slim legs. Her feet were aching furiously from the strain of rough hiking in ordinary shoes. They no longer had the energy to hurry.

The ground was a lot more even as they went along, and it was apparent that they had left the flank of the mountain. It lurked black and menacing behind them but they did not look back. The sound of the sea grew slightly further away and they realized that the rugged coastline was curving away from them. The mist was thinning a bit and then suddenly Larry saw the dim outline of the lift machinery of the mine much further inland and crowning the brow of a hill to their left.

He stopped and pointed out the outline of the hoist. It was above them and almost a quarter mile inland. They turned towards it before the mist clamped down on them again and then followed the general direction away from the sea. They moved cautiously now, knowing that the old workings lay between the modern mine and the sea. They didn't want to find their way into the old galleries by plummeting down some unknown shaft hidden in the hillside.

The ground began to rise steeply — a sharp grass-covered gradient that rose for over a hundred yards before easing off a little. They scrambled up it slowly, eyes and ears alert for any sign of a trap. The thick mist was a mixed blessing and a curse. It would hide them from any watchers, but it would also hide the watchers from them. They made little or no sound on the wet grass and moved almost silently. Then the square shape of a building loomed ahead and beyond it the tall outline of the hoist.

They moved in almost up to the buildings and crouched low behind a tumble of boulders. They could make out more buildings now, half a dozen of them. Above them all loomed the hoist, squatting over the main shaft to the mine workings. In silence they watched and waited. There was a small square of light in one of the buildings and it was this that held their attention. After a while a door beside the lighted window opened and a man stepped out. Beside him was a police constable, and in the room they could just make out the shape of a second blue uniform. One of the two said something to the man inside and then closed the door. The first man out, obviously a nightwatchman of some kind, produced a torch to light their way. The policeman followed him.

They watched as the two men made a brief trip around the mine buildings and then returned to where they started. The nightwatchman said something at which they both laughed. They went back inside and the constable slammed the door.

Larry murmured quietly, 'Do you think that's all?'

Linda frowned. 'I think it must be. I can't really imagine them filling the place with hidden detectives. They've ordered the local police to keep an eye on it and the main road and that's about it. The main search for you is probably still concentrated further south. At least it will be until that car load you ran off the road get in to report.'

'Then we'd better get going before those guys in the hut make their rounds again.'

They closed in on the mine and drew up in the shadows of the nearest building. The hoist was still some fifty yards away. Here he stopped and pointed to a long wooden hut that had the words MAIN OFFICE painted above the door. 'That's our first port of call,' he said softly. 'We need a plan of the workings to find our way underground. We could search for days in that maze of tunnels without them. We need lights of some kind too.'

She said tensely, 'What about the guards?'

'We'll have to risk them. With luck they'll stay by the stove in that hut until they have to make the rounds again. You keep an eye on them.'

She nodded and they crossed swiftly to the office. Here Linda watched the lighted hut from the shadows while Larry hunted for something to force the single office window. He found a heap of junk nearby and amongst it an old broken file. He returned smiling to tackle the window.

The point of the file was broken short but the wood of the flimsy window frame was soft. He started breaking away slivers of wood near the catch and it splintered easily. After ten minutes vicious twisting he had broken enough away to insert the file and lift the simple catch. The window came open easily.

He called Linda over and helped her quickly through the window. There was a large desk-cum-table on the other side and she knelt on it to help haul him up. He wriggled in, face down beside her, and then turned on one hip to shut the window behind him. Together they dropped on to the floor.

He said softly, 'You know, we'd make a good team of cat burglars.' She smiled silently in the darkness and he went on, 'Now let's see what we can find.'

11

Into the Mine

It was pitch black inside the small office
and for a few moments they stood there
undecided, then Linda produced a box of
matches and struck one to enable them
to see. The dim, wavering light showed
them a high steel filing cabinet and a
pair of straight-backed chairs. There was
a tall cupboard in the corner, and on
the walls were some schedule sheets, a
pin-up calendar and three large drawings
that showed the layout of the tunnels in
the mine. Larry moved towards the latter
as the match fizzled out.

'Another match,' he whispered.

He heard the rasp of a match on the
box and then the dim light flared again.
Linda held it closer to the drawings.
Two of the plans were of the levels of
the recent tunnels still being worked,
the lines of the galleries clear and easy

to follow. The third map traced the haphazard labyrinth of the old mine.

Swiftly Larry took the third map from the wall. Blackness engulfed them again and he waited impatiently while Linda struck a third match. When it was alight he swiftly extracted the map from its frame. He turned to the other two plans and saw that on the one of the lowest level were several red shaded tunnels that connected up with the old workings. All were marked unsafe and blocked. Larry took that map too.

He folded the maps and stuffed them into his jacket and then carefully replaced the frames on the wall. If the nightwatchman shone his torch through the window after they left he might not notice that the frames were empty, whereas he most certainly would notice them if they were left on the floor.

Their next and more important objective was a couple of miner's helmets with lights, and again they were lucky first time. In the tall cupboard in the corner Larry found several sets of clean overalls, some pairs of sturdy hob-nailed boots, and most important of all, three helmets sitting on the top shelf. He gave Linda a swift smile of relief. Then carefully he took down two of the helmets just as the last match went out, and closed the door in darkness.

'No more matches,' he told her. 'It's time we got out.'

In silence they felt their way back across the room to the window. Larry climbed on the large desk and peered through the glass. The night was silent and still. Cautiously he opened the window and glanced out. There was nothing to be seen or heard.

He turned to give Linda a hand up on to the table and then thrust his legs through the open window and pushed himself out. He landed upright and then turned back to lift her down. Pushing the window shut they moved to the edge of the building where they could see the hut where the nightwatchman and the two constables sheltered. The light was still on but there was no movement from inside.

Larry gripped Linda's hand and said

softly, 'Come on.'

Crouching low they ran across the open space in the circle of the buildings to the pithead.

They reached the dense shadows beneath the outline of the hoist and passed through an unlocked door into the high shed that housed the lift cage. Again they were in pitch blackness once they closed the door, and after a few minutes in which they regained their breath Linda risked striking another match.

They moved swiftly, ignoring the lift cage and searching round behind it for a ladder that would take them down into the mine. Even if they could have started the hoist machinery and got the cage going it would have made far too much noise. They circled the railed-in entrance to the shaft and then found what they were looking for. A gate in the rails and beyond the head of a steel runged ladder leading down to the depths.

There was a padlock on the gate but they easily climbed over. The match went out as Larry helped to steady Linda as she stepped down.

'Helmets on,' he said quietly. 'We'll light them up the moment we get below ground level.'

He fitted his own helmet and waited until she had adjusted hers. He felt for the head of the ladder with his hands and breathed a sigh of relief as he found it. It rose waist high out of the shaft and he swung out on it nervously, his foot clanged slightly as he kicked the rungs before becoming firmly anchored. Leaning forward he found Linda's arm and guided her hand on to the ladder head. Climbing down he found her ankle in the darkness and helped guide her foot on to the rung above his head.

'Okay,' she said quietly. 'I can manage.'

They descended into the depths, moving slowly, feeling their way down the steel rungs of the ladder. It was frightening to be swinging down into the inky blackness of the shaft. Very frightening. It only needed one slip to plunge them hundreds of feet into the bowels of the earth. Hurtling down to shatter on the unseen floor below. The steel rungs were ice-cold to their hands but they hardly noticed.

Larry stopped at last and heard Linda come to a halt a few rungs above him.

'Let's get some light,' he said. 'Nobody could notice it now.'

He fumbled with the lamp in his helmet and switched it on. The beam of light hit the shored-up walls of the shaft and bounced back in his eyes. The sudden transformation almost blinded him and he had to blink sharply for a few moments before his vision returned. He looked up then and the light from his helmet illuminated Linda as she switched on her own. She looked down at him and smiled.

'That's better,' she said. 'A lot better. Coming down here in the dark made my heart race away like a Derby winner. It's not so bad when you can see.'

They looked around them slowly. The wide shaft was well shored up but in places bare earth and rock showed through gaps in the planking. On either side of the shaft ran runners to steady the lift cage in its descent. Below them the steel rungs of their ladder vanished into the gloom. Everywhere was still and silent.

Determinedly they continued down, step after step until it seemed that the pit shaft must descend for ever. Then at last, when their arms and legs were aching with the strain, they came upon the first level of the mine workings. The ladder passed through a narrow platform that led to the high openings of the tunnels on either side. They moved round the platform thankfully and rested in the mouth of one of the tunnels. Behind them a line of narrow coal trucks stood on a small gauge set of tracks that led away into the blackness of the mine.

Linda said wearily, 'Oh, my aching legs!'

Larry smiled. 'It's only another fifty feet down. The plan we left behind must be this level, and that was marked one hundred and fifty feet. The bottom level was marked two hundred.' He pulled his stolen maps from his jacket and spread them out. 'Let's have a good look at these now. No one will interrupt us down here.'

'Suppose there's a night shift below?' she asked.

'I very much doubt it. There's no sign of movement and in this isolated area I doubt if they can get enough labour to run two shifts.' He frowned and went on, 'I did expect to find some one down here though. According to the last paper I read the police were still trying to break through one of the blocked tunnels that lead to the old workings. It's a certainty that they'll keep on until they do get through.'

'There was nothing about it in today's papers. But I suppose they could have broken through after the papers went to press. In fact that would explain why there's no activity either above or below.'

Larry said slowly, 'In that case we can get through behind them. They'll have removed the bodies but there must be something there that will tell us what happened. Perhaps just being there again will jolt my memory.'

'It might do, but if the police are still working at clearing that tunnel, how do you expect to get in then? There's no other way. If there was, the police would have found it by now.'

'I've thought of that,' he said. 'If there's no way into the old workings, then we'll hide in the mine until they do break through. I don't believe it's possible for us to get there first, but at least I'm going to get there. That old mine holds all the answers and I've got to get in.'

Linda looked thoughtful. 'It's now Friday night,' she mused. 'They've been at it since dawn Monday so even if they aren't through they must be getting very close.'

'I think they must be through,' he said. 'But one way or the other I'm going on.' He unfolded the two maps and spread them side by side on the rough surface of the tunnel floor. He knelt over them and Linda knelt beside him, the combined lights from their helmets lit everything up clearly.

The main pit workings were clear broad lanes that spread mostly inland from the shaft beside them. Only half a dozen or so travelled seawards in the direction of the original mine, these all branching from two main galleries from the shaft. Three of the six broke into the old workings but in each case the tunnels were marked as blocked for several hundred yards after the old part of the tunnels began. They knew it must be one of those three tunnels that the police were attempting to clear, or had already cleared.

They fitted the map of the old mine against the edge of the new, following the lines of the blocked tunnels into the wavering maze that marked the original workings. The galleries splayed out like the spokes of a wheel from the main shaft that had been marked with a cross. That was the shaft where Larry had been hauled up bleeding and half insane. One of the spokes ran in a crazy wavering line to the west, far under the sea. The others branched out in all directions and thrust out small criss-cross tunnels in all angles. The whole effect was rather like looking at the skeletons of half a dozen leaves, their thick roots all merging at the base of the shaft.

They studied the maps for several minutes, then Linda remarked, 'Well, providing it's possible to get through, we should find our way all right.'

Larry nodded. 'Our way should be clear enough, as long as we don't stray out of it. I should hate to get lost in the maze of the old mine.' He began refolding the maps and went on. 'Now all we have to do is find out which of those three possible tunnels the police were trying to clear. If they've already got through we can get to the base of the old shaft tonight. If not we hide in the mine until they do.'

They straightened up and Linda asked, 'Do you really think we'll be safe down here? Tomorrow morning they must find out that the office was broken into, and after that police car we ran off the road they know we're in the area. They'll be sure to connect the two and realize it was us.'

'I still don't think they'd expect us to hide in the mine. I'm going to chance it anyway. Now that I've come this far I'm certainly not going back until I've been to the foot of that shaft. I've got to know whether I killed those men — and there must be something there that will tell me.'

There was a catch in his voice that made Linda lay gentle fingers on his arm.

'You didn't kill them, Larry, I've already told you that.'

'No? Then what did I shoot at down there?'

'I don't know. Perhaps it was — was whatever clawed at your face.'

Larry felt suddenly cold. 'What makes you so sure it was something with claws?'

'Again I don't know. But those long slashes down your face were not caused by the falling shaft, Larry. Something did that before the shaft came down.'

Larry swallowed slowly then said, 'Linda I don't like it. I know there's danger down there somewhere. I can't remember what but I know there's something. Something deadly. I wish you'd go back up and wait for me.'

She said softly, 'Larry, the last time you were down there you almost died, and you almost lost your sanity. You'll need a friend beside you when you find out why. You'll need me.'

He knew that there was no point in arguing with her. Her mind was made up.

He said grimly, 'Okay then, let's go.'

They finished the last fifty feet to the bottom of the shaft with comparative ease. Here there was a concrete floor where the lift cage rested and on either side wide tunnels led off into the blackness. Steel rails ran into the gloom and on the left-hand track a string of trucks, loaded high with gleaming coal, were pulled up near the shaft. There was complete silence in the mine, and it was frightening to realize that there were hundreds of feet of solid rock and earth above them.

Larry took Linda's arm and led her along the left-hand tunnel towards the old workings. Their helmet lights cast vague shadows as they walked and the sound of their steps was alarmingly loud. Linda pressed close to Larry's side.

They came to a point where the tunnel split into two branches and

Larry unhesitatingly took the right fork, remembering from his map that two of the blocked tunnels to the old mine were in that direction. The tunnel roof became lower as they walked. The walls were shored up with planks and the roof supported by stout pit props of knotted pine, their peeled surfaces black with coal dust.

Fear began to curdle in Larry's stomach as they penetrated further into the depths of the earth. They were walking into danger he was sure. He could remember nothing, yet he was sure of it. It was cold down here but his palms and temples were greasy with sweat. The feeling grew stronger with every step and his face began to pain him in a sudden agony of warning. A nameless terror gripped his heart and he wanted to turn and run.

They passed a left fork and soon after came to a second. Here Larry checked his map and then turned off in the new direction. The tension was tightening within him as he followed the slightly narrow tunnel towards the old mine workings. After three to four hundred yards the tunnel ended in a barrier of old boards and a red painted sign with the one word: DANGER. Beyond the boards the tunnel was completely blocked.

Larry turned away from the boards, his mouth tight and strained against its frame of bandages.

'We go back and take the next left fork along,' he declared. 'Nobody's tried to open this tunnel for years.'

They retraced their steps back to the main tunnel and moved on again. To Larry the moving shadows just beyond the range of their helmet lamps took on a weird, sinister, aspect. His nerves were at full stretch now and every step was fraying at his self-control. He knew now why he needed Linda beside him. Without her he would have broken and run back.

The black mouth of the next branching tunnel suddenly loomed on their left and they followed the side track of the steel rails into it. Larry felt the sweat trickle down his spine, it was warm but the damp trail seemed to freeze as it passed.

Then abruptly they saw more boards ahead.

He went right up to the boards and peered through a gap. The tunnel went on beyond the boards. Once it had been blocked, but now it was cleared and the boards replaced.

He said hoarsely: 'This is it. They've been through here.'

'Then they must have got through. They wouldn't have boarded it up and left it without recovering the bodies.'

He nodded and began tearing at the boards. They came away easily and he threw them behind him. The noise as they hit the steel rails clanged loudly in the silence. He didn't notice. He tore the last board away with fumbling hands and stepped beyond the barrier. He turned to help Linda through, his heart beating wildly.

'Come on, let's see what they found.'

She took his hand again and they hurried on. Here the roof had been shored up with fresh white props, clear evidence that this part of the tunnel had recently been unblocked. Then, a hundred yards further on, the cleared length ended. The tunnel narrowed by half and the props that shored up the walls were rotten with mould. There were no longer any rails and the surface was rough rock and earth. They were in the old workings of the McArnot mine.

Larry hesitated, his torn face still paining him in silent warning. Then he started on into the old mine, the girl staying close by his side. The tunnel floor sloped down steeply for several yards, the walls closing in on them all the time. They went down the slope, their lights picking out rotten timbers half falling from the walls. The gallery smelt of age and rot and the whole atmosphere was one of decay. They walked for perhaps fifty yards into the old mine and then, without warning, they stepped ankle-deep into ice-cold water.

They glanced downwards together and came to a halt. Ahead stretched a silent rippling river of water. Black water that went on and vanished into the old mine.

The lower galleries of the old mine were flooded.

12

Black Waters

The sight of that dark, unmoving, surface of water flooding the ground level of the mine, made Larry forget his fears and recoil stunned with shock. The little ripples around their feet died and the black river gleamed faintly in the light of their lamps. They stared at it without quite grasping its meaning. And then Linda said unnecessarily:

'It's flooded.'

Larry regained control of his scattered thoughts but was still too stunned to speak. All that way for this. He felt as though he had walked into a trap, a mesh of close, invisible coils that kept him helpless and afraid. It was like waking up again to the silent darkness of the nursing home. Knowing nothing and with no hope. He cursed bitterly. He had been so sure and had relied so much on finding all the answers to his past in this old mine. And now it was flooded, the icy water lapping around his ankles and chilling his feet. He cursed again, slowly, bitterly, with no thought. Just futile words against a harsh fate.

Linda still held his hand. She said softly, very softly, 'Don't despair, Larry. We'll find the answers — somehow.'

'How?' His voice was toneless.

'I don't know — but somehow.'

He stared down the dark river, his free hand knotted into a fist at his side.

He said suddenly, 'It wasn't flooded before. It couldn't have been. Where did it come from?'

She remained silent for a moment and then remembered the map. 'There was one gallery stretching out under the sea wasn't there? The sea must have broken in. We must be just about sea level now. The pithead was really high above sea level, easily two hundred feet.'

He stood there silently, as if the water had somehow absorbed all the energy out of his body. He felt weak-kneed and near exhaustion. He had almost forgotten their stiff passage over the mountainside in the thought of nearing his goal. Now the reaction was setting in, swiftly and painfully. He felt stiff and tired, as though every muscle had quit hopelessly in the face of the waterlogged tunnel. Not even his brain was capable of working any more.

Linda said softly, 'This must be what held the police up. That's why there's no more activity down here. They can't get through.'

Larry, his face suddenly grim, burst out angrily, 'I'm going on. May be I can wade through it. The ground might rise further along.'

She wasn't hopeful, but she answered instantly. 'All right, we'll go on.'

'You wait for me here. I'll go on ahead. If it gets too deep there's no point in us both getting soaked. It feels damned cold too. It'll be no pleasure paddle.'

She shivered a little. 'I'll wait for you then, but if you go too far I'm coming after you anyway. I don't want to lose sight of you.'

He didn't argue; he didn't want to lose

sight of her either. He didn't want her to meet up with whatever danger prowled the mine on her own.

He squeezed her hand and said gently, 'I won't go too far. If it looks possible I'll call you on.' He stepped back on to dry land and swiftly took off his jacket and shirt. There was no point in getting his clothing wet as well as his body. He stripped down to his pants and rammed his helmet hard on his head for he couldn't afford to lose it. The musty air became suddenly clammy to his skin. He shivered.

Linda pulled her coat around her. 'Be careful, Larry.'

He gave her a grin that carried more confidence than he was feeling and walked barefoot to the water's edge. The water was cold enough to make him grit his teeth as he stepped into it. He walked out and felt it rise swiftly to his knees. He trembled violently but kept on going.

Linda watched him wade forward, the disturbed water rippling in twin trails from his legs. Her face was pale in the glow of the lamp on her forehead, her eyes filled with worry. She waited with her hands at her sides. She shivered just from watching him.

Larry felt the water rise up to swirl around his thighs. Here, deep in the heart of the mine, there was never any sunlight to warm the water and its temperature was near to freezing. He had waded only two dozen yards and already his legs were numb.

He moved on doggedly and the floor levelled off. He felt new hope and strode on forcefully, the water never rising above his thighs. The sides of the old tunnel were very close in now, barely five feet apart. The roof was only a foot or two above his head, crumbling in places. Once or twice lumps of rock or earth splashed down close to him, kicking up a little flurry of water that sprayed his body. Each one made him shiver uncontrollably.

His teeth were chattering by the time he had made sixty yards and still the tunnel showed no signs of sloping any deeper below sea level. He bit his lip and pushed on. Then suddenly Linda called his name.

He looked back to see her struggling out of her coat, a lonely, dim, figure behind the light of her head lamp. She called again.

'Wait, Larry, I'm coming with you.'

He shivered, opened his mouth to tell her no, and then checked it. He wasn't sure even now whether she would be safer with him or not. He didn't want her to face the ordeal of the freezing water. But he also didn't want to leave her behind. Somehow he was sure that the unknown terror of the mine was by far the one to be most dreaded.

Linda didn't wait for him to answer. She threw her coat down beside his clothes and swiftly slipped out of her skirt and blouse. She kicked off her shoes and moved determinedly into the water. The coldness of it almost made her cry out as she plunged on. She had to bite her lip and hurry forward, the water splashing around her stockinged thighs and the force of it slowing her up.

Larry called back, 'Take it easy, I'm

waiting for you. And mind you don't step into any holes. There's no telling what the surface of this tunnel is really like.'

She came up to him with her face twisted with the pain of her half-frozen legs. She was several inches shorter than he and the water that only reached the tops of his thighs already surged around her hips. He put one arm around her naked waist as she came up and found that her flesh was already cold and clammy.

'You should have stayed behind,' he said tightly.

'I couldn't.' Her teeth chattered as she spoke. 'Come on, let's get going before we freeze.'

They moved on down the flooded tunnel. The shoring on the walls were now crumbling and rotten and once they had to climb over two fallen pit props that had collapsed diagonally across the tunnel. Then slowly the water became deeper, moving up around their hips. It reached Linda's waist and then Larry's. He was leading the way now, moving warily from fear of falling into some unsuspected hole.

Linda said grimly, 'How far is the main shaft? The one that fell in?' Her voice was strangely hollow-sounding.

'About three hundred yards I think.' The fierce cold almost constricted his throat so that he could hardly speak. 'I can't be sure because the map gave no scale, but this tunnel should take us right to it.'

They passed the dark mouth of another branching tunnel where more black water stretched into the distance. Ahead there was still nothing but the black gleam of the sea. It glinted treacherously in the flickering light from their head lamps. As they moved, it stirred sluggishly and slapped against the rotting walls.

The level rose gradually until the surface lapped just below Linda's brassière and played with icy fingers around Larry's chest. The lower part of their bodies were almost without feeling now. It was a blessing but a dangerous one. Soon they would have to turn back or they would probably freeze to death. Larry still kept one arm about Linda's waist, cursing himself for ever allowing her to come. He should have made her wait for him above the ground. He should never have let her into the mine at all.

The ground sloped down abruptly and plunged them in up to their shoulders. The dark water stretched on but there was still a bare two feet between the surface and the crumbling roof. Larry opened his mouth to speak but the cold seemed to have cut off the air in his throat. His mouth gaped open for several seconds before he managed to gasp, 'Wait here, I'll swim on.'

He let his feet come up and struck out powerfully along the tunnel. He realized that the movement would help to keep his circulation going, and pulled himself through the icy water as fast as he could go. Behind him Linda swam in his wake. Unable to speak she was still determined to follow him on. He kept his head high as he swam, trying to keep his bandaged face out of the water. Once a wave splashed in his face, it had a foul taste, stagnant and salty.

For another fifteen to twenty yards they

swam down the flooded tunnel before the low roof dipped abruptly down into the water. Larry swore viciously, or rather tried to, for the words jammed in his constricted throat. They must almost be up to the surface shaft they were trying to reach. Another fifty yards or so would be enough. Only from here on, the whole of the old mine workings were full of sea water.

Larry stared at the point where the surface and tunnel roof met, and then turned bitterly away. Linda's cheeks were blue with the cold and he realized from his own numb limbs that even now they might freeze before they could get back along the flooded tunnel and out of the old mine. He could no longer speak and he had to jerk his head to indicate that he was going back. She turned and he swam strongly in her wake. Both were only too eager now to regain the drier lengths of the tunnel and moved vigorously without any thought of caution.

They kept on swimming long after they regained their own depth, for that way they were moving faster and their energetic kicking was helping to combat the fierce cold that ate into their bodies. The tunnel roof rose gradually higher above them, the shadows beneath it playing crazily in the jerking light of their head lamps. They swam on, no longer aware of anything but the need to get out of the freezing waters. Larry had even forgotten his fears of the unknown terror that lurked in the old galleries.

Linda suddenly lurched to her feet ahead of him and he realized that they were back in waist-deep water. She staggered forwards and fell with a splash as he found the bottom and floundered towards her. He picked her up and found with a shock that he couldn't feel her. If he hadn't seen his hands around her waist, helping her upright, he would have sworn that he had not touched her. He pulled her to him and hustled her on. She was a limp weight in his arms, with no will left to help herself. Her feet dragged uselessly behind her.

They came back to the side tunnel that branched off into nowhere. Larry hardly noticed it, splashing past until abruptly another splash sounded above his own. Terror gripped him in a vice of steel and he whirled in the waist-deep water to face the tunnel mouth. He had heard that warning splash before — before he had lost his memory.

The swinging light of his head lamp picked out a pair of eyes. Dark beady little eyes that gleamed and glittered, surging towards him through a dark V of ripples. The eyes were close set in a pointed skull, sharp little teeth flashed white in the long bared jaws.

Larry knew then why he had been afraid. The sight of that deadly little body bearing down on him through the black waters snapped open the flood gates of his mind and his memory came back in a flash of horror. Too late he realized the deadly danger he had brought Linda into.

He pushed the girl aside as the rat shot for his throat, for a rat it was, a sleek hefty rat almost two feet long. The razor-edged teeth lunged for his throat as he brought his hands up and made a grab for its neck. The jaws snapped and tore a shred of flesh from the side of his thumb as he closed his grip. His hands were so numb that he didn't feel it. The force of the brute carried him staggering backwards and the bright glittering eyes flashed into his own. He squeezed the slippery neck in his hands, crushing the life out of the brute as it fought to get at him. He felt its clawing forepaws slash at his wrist and then black fury rose within him. He saw Linda staring in horror as she hung on to the rotten wall of the tunnel for support, and the thought of the danger to her drove him into the rage of a maniac. He swung his arms up lifting the heavy body clear of the water and swinging round in a circle he smashed its head against the side of the tunnel.

The rat squeaked in pain and its claws raked the air futilely. It fell back into the sea with a splash, Larry's hands still clamped about its throat. He lifted it again, fear for the girl spurring him on, savagely he smashed the pointed head against a sagging pit prop. He smashed at it again and the prop buckled and collapsed. He dug his thumbs into the dying rat's throat and choked the last remnants of life from its ugly body.

He lifted the corpse high and hurled it far up the flooded tunnel. Without a pause he splashed over to Linda and pulled her away from the wall.

'Come on,' he shrieked hoarsely. 'We've got to get out.'

He hustled her along the tunnel, fighting his way frantically through the weight of water that held him back. Fear spurred him on. Fear of what he had remembered when the rat sprang out of the darkness. There was a whole pack of the great rats somewhere in the old mine.

The girl was a half-frozen burden in his arms and he abruptly lifted her high, clear of the water. She clung to him weakly and he pressed on, kicking his way through the pressure of the sea against his legs. He came to the fallen pit props that lay across the tunnel and savagely kneed them aside. The rotten wood splintered and gave way beneath the force of his knee and he splashed on, his legs were too numb to feel pain.

The depth of the water began to lessen and he broke into a sluggish run. He wanted to look back but he daren't. He prayed that the rest of the pack lurked deeper in the flooded tunnels. Linda's body was wet and violently trembling in his arms.

His foot slipped as he ran through knee-deep water and he staggered and almost fell. Regaining his balance he sprinted on, water cascading up before his legs. The depth lessened to a mere foot and he ran even faster, the water spraying high up the dank walls. Then suddenly there was dry ground beneath his feet and he stumbled to a halt.

He collapsed on his knees before their pile of clothes and clumsily bundled them on top of Linda. He straightened up and began running again. Away from the old mine and back into the new workings. His bare feet were cut and bruised in a dozen places but he never gave them a thought. He ran back through the unblocked tunnel and retraced their path back to the main surface shaft. Not until he was there did he stop.

His chest was heaving like a set of giant bellows as he gasped for breath. He set Linda's feet on the ground and swayed in near exhaustion. He was warmer now, his terror-filled race through the mine having restarted the circulation in his blood. He sucked in great mouthfuls of air and then abruptly he realized that Linda was still only a limp weight against him.

He pushed her away, holding her at arms length and trying to hold her straight. Water still trickled down her naked flesh, and her body was a bluish grey with the cold. She was only just conscious.

'Linda, Linda can you stand?' His voice was broken with anguish and sounded cracked and shrill in the stillness of the mine.

She nodded and abruptly her teeth began to chatter noisily.

He stopped and grabbed up his shirt from the pile of clothing at their feet. She almost fell into the curve of his left arm and he began to rub furiously at her back. His frenzied pummelling snapped the strap of her sodden brassière and the garment fell unheeded to the ground. He worked fast, desperately trying to massage some warmth into her half-frozen body. Her teeth kept chattering and the sound almost drove him to despair.

When he turned her round her face was still blue with cold. Her full breasts might have been carved from cold slippery marble. He kept on rubbing her vigorously until at last he brought a red flush to her skin, she began to look more alive and was able to steady herself while he rubbed some colour into her arms.

'Th-thanks, Larry,' she managed to shudder. There was still no colour in her face.

He forced a grin. 'You'll be okay, don't worry.' He picked up her blouse and helped her put it on. She did up the buttons with stiff, clumsy, fingers. She stood still then, apart from an occasional fit of shuddering. Holding herself in check while he knelt and peeled the sodden stockings from her legs. He massaged her thighs and calves until they too lost their grey clammy texture. She was still shivering then but at least in no more danger of freezing. She managed to get her skirt on with only a limited amount of help.

He made her wrap herself up in her grey overcoat and then did his best to dry and dress himself. She was still shivering when he finished and he ordered her firmly to start moving about. She made a dull effort and then shook her head. She was still too stiff and numb to help herself.

Grimly he moved behind her and gripped both her wrists. He made her swing her arms back and forth as hard as he could go. The exertion warmed them both and after a while she was able to work without his support and help. He made her work her legs then, bringing her knees up one at a time in some brisk running on the spot. At one point it struck Larry as slightly ridiculous that they should be doing solemn physical exercises deep below the earth. But there was no one to see them and he made the girl carry on until they were both feeling alive again.

At last even the agony as the blood circulated in their fingers and toes passed and they stopped to catch their breath. Linda complained that only her breasts still hurt, but apart from that she was feeling fit. She managed to give him a smile and this time it was the full-lipped smile of old, not a mere twist of a grey mouth and slack cheeks.

She went on quietly, 'I'm only sorry it was all for nothing Larry. If only we could have found something it wouldn't have mattered.'

He laughed suddenly. 'But we did. That rat did it. It was one of those that tore my face. The sight of it brought it all back.' He sobered suddenly and said flatly, 'I can remember how those three men died, Linda.'

She saw a lost, haunted look appear in his eyes and instinctively she moved closer against him. As if to give him courage her hand closed on his arm.

He met her eyes slowly and said, 'It's true what the police think. I shot them. I killed all three.'

13

How Three Men Died

Linda was stunned at his sudden admission. For a moment she faltered uncertainly, and then she moved closer to him. She said quietly, 'Do you want to tell me about it?'

Her reaction gave him new heart. He said, 'Do you feel fit enough to climb up to the next level? I'll tell you the full story there. I've seen enough of this part of the mine.'

She shuddered. 'Me too. I don't want to see any more of those horrible brutes.'

'They're not normal rats,' he explained. 'They're a large, almost extinct breed of South American water rat; one of the most vicious and dangerous breeds alive.'

'Tell me later. Right now I want to get out of here.'

He nodded and let her lead the way up the shaft. He kept close behind her as she climbed in case she was still numb from the cold and wet. However she seemed to have fully recovered and they reached the next level without incident. Here Linda bandaged his torn thumb with a part of the silk slip she still had in her pocket. For a moment as she worked she became again the efficient capable nurse he had first known.

Finally she said, 'That will keep it clean for you. Now we can rest here while you tell me what you remembered.'

She slipped out of her grey coat so that they could both sit inside it and snuggled up against him as they leaned against the wall.

He began: 'There were six of us in the party that went down into those old workings. Lucas, the assistant mine manager, Mason, his secretary, Neal and Vickers, a couple of miners, Crane, the mine foreman, and myself.'

'Then Crane was one of them!' Linda ejaculated.

'He was one of them all right.' Larry

grimaced and began again. 'I was a freelance journalist. I came here to write an article on the fishing boats that sailed from Shieldonnel when the west gallery on the lower level of this mine fell in. I had only been here a few hours and hadn't even booked in at a hotel by then, which explains why nobody knew me. However when I heard about the pit fall I came rushing straight over. I figured I had a better story at my finger-tips.

'As you know I approached Lucas and asked him if I could go along when he and the others went down into the old workings. There was a lot of equipment bottled up by the fall and Lucas believed that it might be easier to break through from the old workings, which ran close to the west gallery, than to clear the fall itself. Our job was to inspect the workings and see if they were safe.'

'We had to descend by ropes because the old ladders in the shaft had rotted away. Only parts of the tunnel were flooded then, mostly those on the seaward side and they were only a few feet deep. I guess the old gallery that stretches under the sea must have caved in since then. Anyway we had a good look round to check the props and shoring where the men would have to work and then came back. Lucas had decided to go ahead once he had the supports strengthened. Neal and Mason went first up the rope and it was then that I found the pack.'

'You mean the rats?' Linda's voice still held a note of fear.

'No, this was an old haversack, green with mould and lying under the surface up one of the flooded galleries. The surroundings were all new to me and I was doing a little private wandering around away from the shaft. I could just make out the shape of this haversack and waded up the tunnel to fish it out. That was what started all the trouble, that was why Crane went crazy — or a least he seemed crazy at the time.'

He paused to straighten the events out in his own mind and Linda waited patiently, letting him set his own pace.

He went on, 'I brought the pack back to where the other three were waiting for their turn to go up. I remember Lucas was a little angry because I had strayed away. He said the mine was dangerous. I gave him the haversack then and that was when Crane went barmy. I hadn't taken much notice of him before. He was a surly type and I think he rather resented Lucas for having let me come. Anyway Lucas just turned the thing over in his hands. It was heavy and thick with slime and green and he was a bit reluctant to touch it. Vickers said should he open it and Lucas gave it to him. He said, 'We'll take it up top with us and open it there. If there's anything inside we'll hand it over to the police.'

'That was when Crane spoke up. He just said, 'You'll give it to me' in a very cold, hard voice. And when we looked round he was holding a gun.'

Larry halted again at the memory and pulled the grey coat closer about them. Then he continued:

'Lucas seemed as though he didn't believe it at first. He started to move forward and then Crane just lifted the gun and told him to stand still. Lucas stopped and then Crane told Vickers to

230

hand over the haversack. Vickers did as he was told and then Lucas wanted to know what the hell Crane thought he was playing at.

'I think Crane was as unsure about things as we were then. He'd acted mostly on impulse and didn't quite know what to do next. He said he had been searching for that haversack for months and he was damned if he was going to lose it now. I think he was almost tempted into shooting me on the spot because I had stumbled on the damned thing. He didn't tell us what was in it but we gathered it was worth a hell of a lot to him. It must have been, for him to contemplate murder rather than lose it.'

Linda said slowly, 'You mean he meant to murder all three of you, just over that old haversack?'

'That — and what was in it. I believe that if he'd stopped to think things over before pulling his gun he would have let us have the pack. But once he drew that gun on us he'd more or less rushed himself into a dead end. He had to get rid of us then, otherwise he would have had a hell of a lot to answer when we got back to the surface. He wasn't a very bright sort of a man and to him murder was the only answer. He might have got away with it too. His scheme was practically perfect, and no one would suspect murder where there was no apparent motive. Even we didn't know what his motive was, except that he wanted that old haversack.

'His murder plan was pretty simple. He meant to herd us into a dangerous stretch of tunnel that was on the point of collapsing at any time, and then fire a couple of shots into the roof to bring it down. It would have made a neat accident. He told us all about the rats then, saying that he could claim he had been defending himself from them if the shots were heard up above. It seems that they escaped from a private zoo owned by somebody named Colonel Marnoch. Crane said that they originally came from South America, so I think they must be a distant relation to the coypus that breed so easily in this country. There are dozens of those running wild around the Norfolk Broads, so really it's not so remarkable that their cousins have managed to breed here. Only these are a vastly more savage breed than the coypus, and a dozen times as dangerous.

Linda shuddered, then said, 'What eventually happened?'

'I jumped Crane,' Larry told her simply. 'It was a suicide attack, but I was lucky. Once I realized that Crane meant every word he said there was no other choice. Even if he got me I figured that Lucas and Vickers might get out of it. If we waited for Crane to move first none of us were going to get out.

'Crane started walking us towards that stretch of tunnel that he meant to improvise as our grave. On the way we passed a broken-off pit prop sticking out from the wall. We had to duck to get under it and I realized that as Crane followed us he would have to take his eyes off us for a second as he lowered his head. I timed my move just right and swung round on him just as he was ducking under. He tried to bring the gun up but I twisted it out of his hands before

233

he could fire. That was when we fought, we crashed back into that narrow tunnel, kicking and clawing like wild beasts.

'The tunnel was too narrow for either Lucas or Vickers to do anything to help so I had to fight him alone.'

Larry paused in his tale as the vivid memory of those desperate moments filled his mind. Crane had been a big man, powerful and hefty, and it was all Larry could do to hold him down. The gun had been kicked back the way they came and Crane writhed his way towards it with Larry still on top of him. Vickers and Lucas had wavered behind them, unable to reach Crane while he was underneath. Larry drove his fist repeatedly into the big man's face without effect as Crane concentrated on the gun. Larry saw his hand reach towards the weapon and acted desperately. He lurched almost upright and flung himself forwards, he crashed down on Crane and snatched up the gun all in one movement.

Crane went berserk. He butted his head into Larry's stomach and used his greater strength to hurl him aside. Now that Larry had the gun his only aim was to batter the smaller man to a pulp. He caught Larry's collar and half hauled him to his feet before smashing him several yards up the tunnel. Vickers saw his chance and rushed the big man only to be knocked aside. Crane charged at Larry, his big face twisted with rage. Larry lifted the gun point-blank at the big man's chest. Crane still came rushing blindly on.

'No, Crane! Crane you crazy devil!' Larry recalled his shouted words as Crane made his suicide charge. His finger was already closing on the trigger as he spoke but somehow the words had effect. Crane blundered to a halt as Larry hesitated on the trigger. Then slowly he backed up and lifted his hands.

Linda said quietly, 'What happened, Larry?'

He remembered her presence beside him. 'I eventually got the gun,' he said. 'Crane was coming at me like a maniac when I shouted those words you heard when I knocked you down. I was afraid

I was going to have to shoot him.'

He had to stop them and push the memory of that fight from his mind. It was only that and the giant rats that he could clearly remember. He had to make an effort to visualize the rest.

He continued: 'We marched Crane back to the foot of the main shaft. Lucas picked up the haversack and said he was going to open it there and then. He wanted to know what was in it which made it worth three men's lives to Crane. We stood around and watched him as he tried to open it. I was still covering Crane with the gun. Lucas kept fiddling with the straps on the haversack but the metal buckles were thick with rust and he couldn't budge them. He started looking round for something he could snap the straps with. That was when he trod on the nest. He walked a little way up one of the tunnels and then suddenly his foot just vanished into a hole against the wall. He fell down on his face and then he screamed — '

Larry didn't realize that he had stopped talking as he relived those last terror filled moments in the old mine. Vickers had ran forward to help the mine manager to his feet. Lucas screamed again and rolled away from the wall, his foot came out of the wide hole and with it a giant rat. The rodent's razor teeth were buried in the calf of the unfortunate man's leg. Vickers let out a yell of alarm and lashed out with one booted foot. He kicked the rat away and it landed crashing against the tunnel wall. The brute came back squeaking and leapt on to Vickers's chest, knocking the man down.

Larry ran forward, forgetting Crane, even forgetting the gun in his hand. He followed Vickers's actions and booted the brute back into the tunnel. Vickers's face was torn and bleeding but he got to his feet without help. Between them they got Lucas to his feet and helped the man limp back to the shaft.

Crane had gone.

They stared about them and then heard Crane scream. Seconds later he raced back towards them. Three of the large rodents were at his heels. They brought him down within a few yards of the shaft and swarmed over his back. Crane writhed beneath the slashing teeth.

Within seconds the whole mine seemed to be full of rushing furry shapes. Beady eyes glittered in the dark shadows and white teeth flashed. The scent of blood seemed to have aroused them for their leader made straight for Lucas's bloodied leg.

Larry recoiled in horror as the pack closed in. The gun was suddenly useless in his hands for he couldn't fire without risking a bullet finding his companions. Lucas was wrenched screaming off his feet and practically vanished under the pack. Vickers reeled back as another leaping rat sailed at his throat.

There was nothing Larry could do. For a few seconds he was left alone and unscathed as the pack closed in on his blood-streaked companions. He spun round and ran for the dangling rope that hung from the shaft. The gun he stuffed in his belt as he grabbed the rope and began to haul himself up. His feet scrambled at the rotten ladder and kicked through the rungs. He hauled himself hand over hand up the rope and then got a foothold on a firmer rung of the ladder. He looked back as one of the huge rats sprang upwards at his throat.

The heavy body thudded on to his chest and the weight almost tore him from the rope. He swung and jerked like a doll on a string as the rodent clawed at his jacket and found a hold. Bright savage eyes gleamed into his own as he jerked his face aside to avoid the lunging pointed head. White jaws snapped together beside his cheek and he felt the rope burning through his hands as he slid down towards the squeaking pack. He let go with one hand and smashed at the furry horror that clung to his chest. His body was almost horizontal now, one foot still lodged on the ladder rung and one hand sliding down the rope. The rat scrambled higher up his body and he felt the slashing forepaws rake at his face.

He screamed and smashed at the razor-jawed terror with his arm. The jaws snapped again and missed and then raking claws tore again at his face. He struck at the brute again and it fell away, it hung upside down with its hind claws still entangled in the folds of his jacket. He writhed in mid-air, arching his stomach away from the flailing claws that sought to rip out his bowels. With his free hand he seized the brute by the tail and with a surge of terror inspired strength tore it away from him. Half of his jacket went away in its paws as he threw it at the side of the shaft. It splintered the creaking shoring boards and fell back squealing into the pack.

Larry had to grab hold of the rope with both hands to prevent himself following it down head foremost. His foot was still lodged above him on the ladder. He started to pull himself up as the rung gave way and plunged his legs down towards the clamouring rodents. He glanced down as one leapt up and lashed out a savage kick that smashed its jaw and sent it flying back. Desperately he scrambled up the rope, then he felt the rope being pulled up as those on the surface took the strain.

He looked back then. His three

companions were practically buried beneath a dozen of the swarming rats. Crane was already still but the other two writhed and fought, screaming from the impact of slashing teeth. Larry saw Lucas open his mouth in another scream before a furry body blotted out his face. On impulse he dragged Crane's gun from his belt. There was nothing he could do about the greater numbers of the pack but he still could not watch the three men eaten alive. He fired at Lucas's head and saw the man jerk and become still. The echoes of the shot roared through the mine and the rats recoiled for a second before rushing back in. Larry fired again and shot the dying Vickers through the head. He fired a third time into the still form of Crane, feeling sick at the sight of the exposed corpse as the pack backed away for a few brief seconds.

That third shot brought the whole of the rotten shaft crashing around him.

How he hung on to the rope he never knew. The blind instinct to survive gave undreamed strength to his hands and wrists and somehow he clung on.

A falling avalanche of earth and rock thundered around him, all but tearing him from the life-saving rope. He felt himself being dragged up through the barrage that smashed and pounded at his wildly swinging body. A section of the rotten shoring took most of the skin from his left arm with it as it crashed down. His clothing was torn off him and the world was suddenly going black. His last memory was of the rope pulling him ever higher as the force of the avalanche fought to batter him down.

Then the whole world swirled round him like a thick haze of pitch-black smoke, and he knew no more.

14

Again the Stranger

Linda said quietly, 'Go on, Larry, what happened after you overpowered Crane?'

The sound of her voice startled him and he came back to reality. The memory of the three men squirming beneath the rat pack was still fresh in his mind and he shuddered slightly. Her hand closed over his knee in a firm reassuring grip to remind him that she was still there by his side.

'Tell me about it, Larry,' she insisted. 'You can't help yourself by going over and over it in your mind.'

He turned towards her and saw concern reflected in her brown eyes. Her dark curls were awry and some of them were still sticking wetly to her forehead. Her face was pale and troubled and when he thought of how he had almost led her into the same fate as Crane and the others he felt a nausea of horror within his breast. If anything had happened to her — He shuddered again at the thought.

'Please, Larry,' she implored him. 'Don't just think about it. Either tell me or try to push it out of your mind.'

He told her. Slowly, and as briefly as he could. Trying to limit his story to the bare facts and giving no real description of the stark horror as the rat pack attacked. Even so, when he had finished she still could not quell a little shudder of revulsion at the story.

'No wonder you lost your memory,' she breathed slowly. 'I think an ordeal like that would driven most men mad.'

He nodded. 'Even now I can't remember anything between blacking out in the shaft and regaining consciousness in the nursing home in Lincolnshire, over three hundred miles away.'

Her shoulders quivered a little beneath his arm as she answered. 'I doubt if you were ever fully conscious during that time. When they pulled you up and put you in the ambulance you were in such a state of shock that they could get nothing out of you. I did hear Doctor Howell say that three different men had tried to prise that rope out of your hands before they found one with strong enough fingers to pull your hands apart.' She paused and moved her hand on his knee. He covered the hand with his own and she smiled as she went on:

'I think you must have recovered a little once they got you in the ambulance. Your mind was still unhinged and your only thought was to get out and run. It didn't matter where to just so long as you ran away. You must have stowed away then in some southbound lorry that took you down through the highlands and then down the Great North Road. The nursing home was only about eight miles off the A1 and chance must have led you towards it when you left the lorry. You collapsed, utterly exhausted, only a few hundred yards from our gates.'

'I suppose so.' He was a little doubtful.

'Don't worry,' she told him. 'I doubt if you ever will remember exactly what happened on that journey. The important thing is that your memory has returned.'

He smiled a bitter smile that hurt his lacerated cheeks. 'Yes, at least we can thank the fiendish brute that attacked us in the mine for that much. My memory seems to have returned completely apart from that one short period. Only I'm not sure that it's going to do me much good.'

'How do you mean?'

'I mean that I still have to convince the police of the truth of my story. They believe that I'm just an ordinary homicidal maniac. If I turn myself in and tell my story they'll probably smile sympathetically and lock me up in Broadmoor.'

'Oh, no, they couldn't. They — ' She stopped as she realized that it was quite possible.

Larry went on, 'That story about Crane and the haversack will take a lot of believing. And if they don't believe that they're going to be very suspicious about where I got the gun and why I was carrying it. It's going to be very difficult to prove the existence of the rat pack too. Most of them must have drowned when the water rose and flooded the old workings. The one that attacked us was on his own. He might have been the sole survivor.'

'Do you really think he might have been the only one?'

'It's possible. Usually they attack in packs, but there were no others around to hear his squealing. Of course there might be more deeper in the mine. They're water rats and would take a lot of drowning. But if they stay deep in the mine it's going to be just as hard to prove that they exist.' He frowned. 'The whole story sounds so fantastic — that's the real trouble. Everything, right from the moment that Crane pulled that gun, sounds utterly impossible.'

Her brows furrowed in concentration. 'If only we knew what made that old haversack so valuable,' she mused at last. 'Or how it got there? Anything that would help to prove any part of what happened.'

He scowled angrily. 'I thought recovering my memory was my only problem,' he said bitterly. 'I thought that once I knew everything that had happened down in those old workings it would all be finished. Now it seems that I'm wrong. I've only found a lot more questions to answer. Like why Crane wanted that haversack so badly? And how I'm going to convince the police that I'm not making up a pack of fancy lies now that I know they can't check my story?'

'Isn't there any way of reaching that haversack and finding out what was in it? There might be another way into the mine where the tunnels aren't flooded.'

He shook his head. 'The area around that shaft must be flooded, we were sloping down towards it all the while. No, I'm afraid that haversack and all the rest of the evidence is lost for good. We'll never know what that haversack contained.'

'Someone must know, Larry. Someone must have put it there.'

'Perhaps Crane left it there and then mislaid it. He seemed to know what was in it. The only trouble is that he's down there with — ' He stopped then, cursing himself for a blind and senseless fool.

There was one other man who must have known what the pack contained.

Rogart.

Larry had completely forgotten the tall gaunt man who had first told him of the old McArnot mine. There had been no place for the stranger in his thoughts. He had given no consideration at all to the man's desperate need to know what had happened there beneath the earth. He had pushed Rogart deep into the background of his mind. Rogart had been the least of his worries and he had been blindly certain that everything would be cleared up once he had reached the mine anyway.

Now he began to wonder about Rogart.

Who was the man?

Why had he come to the nursing home asking his grimly eager questions?

Why were the possible happenings in the old mine so important to him?

Larry remembered the gaunt man standing over his bed, his clear green eyes gleaming as he talked in his soft Scottish accent. 'I don't see how you could possibly have known what was down that mine until you stumbled across it. With Konrad dead I'm the only man alive who knows it's there.' Those had been Rogart's exact words. And he couldn't have been referring to anything else but that old haversack. It was beyond the realms of possibility that there could be two sources of probable wealth in the same galleries.

He recalled Rogart telling him that he hadn't a hope in hell of making any profit out of his discovery, and then trying to talk him into doing a deal. Rogart had been certain that they had found the haversack. Certain too that Larry had done what Crane had attempted to do: Killed to keep its secrets to himself.

With a thrill of excitement Larry told Linda of his conclusions.

She listened without interruption and then said, 'I think you must have stumbled into a bigger mystery than you thought when you found that haversack, Larry. Crane was willing to kill for it. Rogart believed that you had killed for it. And apparently this man Konrad whom Rogart mentioned had already died for it.'

Larry frowned. 'I'm not so sure. I asked him about Konrad. He just laughed and said the man died of natural causes. Then he added, natural for those times anyway.'

'Even so, it seems that old pack was considered valuable enough to risk committing murder. Both Rogart and Crane thought it was anyway. If only we knew what was in it.'

Larry beat his fist into the palm of his hand, his eyes moody in their frame of dirty white bandages. 'Rogart never gave me a clue as to what might be in it. He just said that he had guessed what I had found and knew why I had murdered those men and then faked a loss of memory. He seemed convinced that that was what was happening. His references to what I had found must have meant that haversack.'

'If the police could trace him they might be able to make him talk. Once he had verified that the pack was valuable enough to make Crane contemplate killing the rest of you it would go a long way towards making the police believe your story.'

Larry said, 'But could they trace him now, after all this time? It's three days since he called at the nursing home and he could be anywhere by now. Rogart didn't strike me as the kind of man who would come forward just to help the police. They'd have to find him.'

'That's true I suppose,' she agreed reluctantly. 'Our chances of finding him are pretty slim. Whatever it is behind all this it's certainly not anything he'd want to discuss with the police.'

'That's right, and where does that leave me? Unless I can convince the police of what really happened in that mine they are still going to regard me as a murderer. They know I was the last man out of the mine and they know I fired three shots at the other three men. I doubt whether they'll ever believe that Lucas and the others were being eaten alive by giant rats.'

'What about this Colonel Marnoch?' Linda suggested. 'The one who owns the private little zoo where these things are supposed to have escaped from. He should be able to confirm your story that the rats exist.'

Again Larry was doubtful. 'Yes, I suppose he would. But even so I don't like the idea of taking my chances with the police in the hope that they'll believe the whole story on the strength of that. They're just as liable to assume that I heard about Marnoch's pets escaping and used the story as a basis for a pack of lies.' He smacked a fist into his palm again, his mouth a tight angry line. 'If only we had some way of reaching that haversack and finding out what was in it.'

They were silent for a few moments, sitting thoughtfully against the wall of the mine with the grey coat wrapped Mexican fashion about their shoulders. The girl was frowning, her brown eyes fixed unblinking on the far wall. Larry's face might have held any expression under the covering of bandages, now smeared with streaks of coal dust. His mouth was still tight but his eyes were blank. Around them there was only the gloomy shadows of the mine, the few coal trucks on the tracks, and the dark massive pit of the shaft to the lower levels.

Linda said suddenly, 'What about a diver, Larry?' There was an eager note in the exclamation. 'Couldn't a frogman swim through those flooded tunnels and reach the haversack?'

Larry sat up abruptly. It was an answer that had not occurred to him but he discarded it almost immediately. 'Where would I get an aqualung and the rest of the equipment?' he asked moodily.

She laughed. 'I didn't mean you. If we tell everything to the police, they could send a frogman down. That haversack must still be where you left it and he could bring it up. Those bodies must be there too. Surely it would be obvious that they had been attacked. It would only need one man to have a good swim round to check your story and everything would be all right. The police would know you were telling the truth.'

Larry looked at her, a little uncomprehendingly. After all his worries it didn't seem possible that it could be that easy. There had to be a flaw somewhere.

'I shouldn't like to send any man down there,' he said.

'Those damned rats could tear him to pieces, even underwater.'

'But there can't be many of them left. You said so yourself.'

'I don't know. The one that attacked us was a lone wolf, but the pack just might be still alive. It's possible that the water rose slowly instead of just rushing in when the tunnel beneath the sea bed collapsed.'

'Even so, a team of frogmen would get through. If several of them went down with spear-guns they could easily defend themselves if they were attacked.' She laughed suddenly. 'You know, I wouldn't mind betting that the police are already planning that anyway. They wouldn't give up all hope of reaching those bodies and finding out what happened without sending divers down to find out. They're probably waiting even now for a team of naval frogmen to come up here and go down there for them. It's the obvious thing for them to do.'

Larry realized abruptly that she was right. The police would undoubtedly send divers down the flooded mine in an attempt to recover the three bodies.

He said grimly: 'Then that settles it, Linda. We'll have to tell the police all we know. We can't let an unsuspecting frogman swim unarmed into the survivors of that rat pack. We'll have to let them know what they're facing so that they can go down well prepared.'

Linda smiled. 'I might have known you'd see it that way.' She gave his knee another gentle squeeze. She went on. 'Once we've seen the police we can forget all about it. They can send divers down to verify your story and we can leave it to them to find the rest of the answers. Even if they don't find them it won't matter to us, just as long as you're in the clear.' She smiled suddenly. 'By the way stranger, what *is* your name? It's about time I knew who I was carrying on with.'

He grinned. 'Like the police say, it's Brown. Plain ordinary Brown. It used to be Douglas — but now it will always be Larry.' On impulse he drew her into his arms and she came willingly. 'I just couldn't answer to anything else any more.'

Her lips were soft and seeking, and her body warm and content as she relaxed in his embrace. Something inside him stirred in a satisfying glow, a tender flame of longing that engulfed them both. He was as good as free now. Free to love her as he had wanted to love her ever since she had found him a name. It had all started from that, and now he could admit it.

At last he broke away. 'Let's get back to the surface,' he said huskily. 'We'll have all the time in the world once we've talked to the police. We'll dump the whole problem in their laps and they can do what they like with it.'

She smiled in agreement and then put her coat back on before starting back up the shaft. Soon the mouths of the tunnels vanished beneath them, above and below there was nothing but the column of steel rungs disappearing into blackness. As they climbed Larry went over everything in his mind but still he could see no snags. Nothing could possibly go wrong.

He was smiling as they finally climbed back into the lift shed. The smile hurt his slashed face but he just felt like smiling. He had his memory, and he had Linda. Nothing could go wrong. Nothing at all.

Then a tall shadow moved out of the gloom of the shed. Larry saw the gleam of green eyes, and thin lips formed in a faint smile. He saw the gun too, in Rogart's hand.

Suddenly he didn't feel like smiling anymore.

15

A Stroll at Gunpoint

Larry heard Linda's little gasp of alarm and felt her stiffen against him. His own heart beat faster and anger boiled up in him. Another few minutes and it should have been over. Just another few minutes. The time it would take to walk over to the hut where the nightwatchman and two constables were on duty.

He took a half pace forward, the skin stretched white across the knuckles of his clenched fist. His eyes glared from his mummified features. Rogart lifted the ugly barrel of the Luger and said curtly:

'That's far enough, Mr. Brown. Now put those headlamps out. Quickly!' The gun lifted. 'And don't try and rush me in the dark, Mr. Brown. I've got cat's eyes. I'll shoot the girl smack in the stomach where it'll make her squirm.'

Larry hesitated.

'The lights, blast you! Switch off those lights.'

Larry switched off his headlamp. Linda did the same, and the interior of the building was plunged into sudden darkness. The effect was blinding. Larry couldn't see a thing. He heard a vague movement ahead and knew that Rogart had changed his position out of caution. He thought that the man had moved to the left but he wasn't sure. In any case he daren't move. Rogart had had plenty of time to let his eyes become used to the darkness before they had climbed out of the shaft. The man could undoubtedly see better than they could, and Larry didn't doubt that he was capable of carrying out his threat to Linda.

Rogart said grimly, 'That's a lot better. Now that trio of fools who are supposed to be watching this place won't see the lights. I only hope they were still busy with their card game while the damn things were on. You ought to have had more sense, Mr. Brown.'

Larry said tightly, 'It didn't matter to

us. We were going over there to give ourselves up anyway.'

Rogart laughed. 'I'll bet you were.'

Their eyes were becoming more accustomed to the blackness now and they could just make out the vague outline of Rogart's figure. Larry still had Linda's hand in his own and he felt her tremble.

She said, 'What are you doing here anyway?'

'Waiting for you.' There was a soft chuckle behind his tone. 'I've been watching the entrance to this mine through binoculars ever since nightfall. I made myself cosy among a little clump of gorse bushes in the rocks further up the hill. You see I had one advantage over the police, I knew you would most certainly make for this spot, whereas they merely thought that you might. They left a couple of men here to keep watch and set up a roadblock or two on the main roads in case you tried to sneak in on the back of a lorry. But it was only as a precaution. They knew nothing definite.'

He chuckled again. 'But we know

different, don't we, Mr. Brown? Though to tell you the truth I didn't expect you for a couple of days yet. You made remarkably good time. In fact, I didn't expect to see the girl either. I thought like everyone else that you must have strangled her some time last night. It never occurred to me that you might have bribed her to help you. How big a cut did you offer her?'

Larry said angrily, 'I don't know what you're talking about.'

'Are you still trying to play that loss of memory game?' The man's tone was taunting. 'I wasn't fooled by that, even at the start.'

'I've recovered my memory.' Larry had to make a real effort now to hold his temper in check. If Linda had not been there he would have thrown himself at the man regardless of the gun. But Linda was there. And he kept remembering Rogart's threat to make her squirm. He finished tautly, 'But I still don't understand what this is all about.'

Rogart was silent for a moment. But when he did speak his tone had changed.

'All right,' he said coldly. 'Let's stop playing games. Where did you find Konrad's pack?'

'If you mean a mouldy old haversack, I have found it. Or at least I know where it is. It's well out of your reach in the flooded galleries of the old mine.'

Rogart drew a long breath. 'Then there's nothing I can do about it at the moment.' The gun lifted again in his hand. 'You'd better be telling me the truth.'

'It's the truth,' Larry retorted savagely, the palms of his clenched fists were beginning to hurt where his nails dug into the flesh. Linda was holding his arm, and her presence did more than the gun to restrain him.

Rogart said grimly, 'All right, we'll discuss it later. Right now we've got to get away from here before those two constables spot us. Those lads may be dumb, but they're not too dumb to understand what goes on under their noses. We'll take a stroll across country to my home and finish our little talk there.'

'You'll never get away with it.' Larry had to unleash his defiance somehow, if only in useless words.

Rogart hissed viciously, 'If you shout like that again I'll really make your sorry. Now move out and remember to keep low. If you deliberately try and let those coppers spot you as we move away I'll kill the girl. I shall be right behind her with this gun at the base of her spine. A bullet there will make her scream so loud it'll make you sick.'

Larry didn't answer. Linda had said several times that he couldn't kill a man in cold blood, but she was wrong. He could kill Rogart easily. He could tear Rogart to shreds with his bare hands.

'Get moving,' Rogart snarled. 'And just remember that I'm right behind her.'

Linda said quietly, 'Take it easy, Larry. There's nothing we can do.'

Larry forced himself to relax. As long as Rogart held that gun on Linda he was in complete command. They had to do exactly as Rogart ordered.

Silently they left the building, and after

a brief glance at the hut where the two police and the watchman were sheltering, Rogart hurried them away from the mine. They climbed over the crown of a steep hill and descended quickly. The outline of the hoist that towered to the sky faded in the thinning mist. Not until they were well clear did Larry risk stopping and turning round.

Rogart halted. A tall shadowy figure in the night. He was wearing a thick, belted, overcoat and the gun in his hand seemed dwarfed by the wide cuff. He said angrily, 'Now what?'

Larry said flatly, 'I want to know what's going on. No one will interrupt us here.'

Rogart laughed. His nerves must have been very keyed up at the mine, for his ruthless manner had dropped away now that they were no longer in danger of being caught.

'Don't worry about it, Mr. Brown. I promise you we'll have a nice long chat once we reach my place. It's too cold to explain here.'

'Whereabout is your place?'

'About three miles from here. We follow the cliffs and then turn inland. You lead the way, and I'll give directions.'

Larry scowled but started moving again. The shrouding mist had lifted slightly but it was still cold and the terrain rugged. Since he had used his shirt as a towel in the mine he had only his jacket and the wind whipped at his bare chest. He shivered as they turned left down a sloping glen that angled down to the coastline and the sea. Loose rocks and shale filled the glen and dark hillsides hemmed them in on both flanks. The ground was very steep and rough and Linda found the going difficult. She tripped and stumbled many times over the grass and heather but Rogart herded them relentlessly along.

Larry helped the girl as best he could, feeling a cold anger towards Rogart hardening in his heart. He had almost got over the bitter disappointment of Rogart's sudden appearance just when it seemed that nothing could go wrong. But his anger was still there, controlled and waiting.

There were a few stars showing above them now, faint glimmers of light against the cloudy darkness. Behind them the rugged outlines of the mountain were etched clear and black in grim silhouette. The wind still moaned through the high crags and slashed fiercely down the glens. From ahead they heard again the crashing of the sea.

They turned left again along the cliff top, heading back below the mine. The sea lay black and sullen on their right, clearly seen now that the mist had faded somewhat. The air was damp with spray. Once Larry glanced back to see Rogart smile and wave him on. He had drawn his right hand into his coat sleeve so that only the deadly nose of the Luger was showing, his other hand was deep in his pocket. He looked very contented and relaxed.

They came suddenly upon a wide track, rutted with the deep wheel marks of heavy lorries. It came down from the mine, now square on their left, and followed the coastline towards the south, away from Shieldonnel cove. They crossed the track and found it wet and muddy. Linda slithered in the mud and Larry had to hold her upright as they picked a path to the firmer grassy ground on the far side.

Rogart said calmly, 'We follow this for a while and then turn inland again. I don't want to follow it out to the road.'

Larry didn't answer him. The only words he had for Rogart would be better said when the man no longer held a gun.

On Rogart's instructions they finally left the track and turned inland. Here they faced rough country of hill and moorland. Once a pair of black-faced sheep ran bleating across their path and made Linda start with alarm. Behind them Rogart laughed cynically. After another mile or so Linda almost fell and Larry had to hold her up. His rage began to slip out of control and he turned on Rogart angrily.

'How much further have we got to go?'

'Another mile or so.' The green eyes were wary.

'Then we'll rest here. She's too tired to go on.'

'Then we'll leave her.' Rogart smiled at his solution. 'But not alive of course. In fact I can't understand why you didn't strangle her long ago. What made you keep her alive?'

Larry glared at the man. Not trusting himself to answer.

Rogart glanced at Linda. 'Well, young lady, are you coming or not? Mr. Brown, I need, but I haven't the slightest use for you. In fact you're a bit of a burden all round.'

'You lousy swine!'

Rogart's gun hand came out of his coat sleeve as Larry snarled the words. He said nothing but the gesture and the expression on his face were enough. His knuckles were white around the gun.

Larry turned and helped the girl on.

They struggled on while Rogart kept several paces behind them. He was taking no chances now and keeping plenty of distance between them. He was well aware of Larry's mood.

Linda was doing her best now to keep

going, but it was clear that she was nearly spent. Her face was pale and her lips trembling. Grimly Larry took her arm over his shoulders and supported her with one arm around her waist. He began to pray for a chance to kill the man behind him.

Suddenly Linda fell and uttered a little cry as she crashed forward. This time she dragged Larry with her and Rogart had to skip nimbly out of the way. His gun trembling in an alert hand.

Larry stopped their rolling progress and got to his knees. Linda lay where she had fallen. For a few moments Larry stared at her without speaking, and then he slowly tunnelled one hand under her knees and lifted her in his arms. She was too exhausted to resist.

Behind them Rogart gave a short, cynical laugh.

Larry clamped his teeth together and struggled on, not trusting himself to speak or look back.

He had to move slowly, picking his way carefully through clusters of gorse and heather. Linda lay limp in his arms.

The rough moorland seemed as though it would never end but finally they came to a road. Larry realized that it had to be the same stretch of road along which he had raced the police car as Rogart hurried them across.

Their way led up yet another steep hillside and the angle of the slope brought Larry's speed down to a series of clumsy lurches. With no free hand to steady himself it took him longer to regain his balance after every step. Behind him Rogart barely concealed his impatience.

Several times Larry thumped down on one knee as he made the last few yards up the hill. When he straightened up on the crest he had to pause for another long breather. Then, below him, he saw the outline of a broad rambling house. It was set in a pocket in the hills and was in total darkness. It was a square, solid, structure with a pair of chimney stacks thrusting short, stubby, fingers to the sky.

Rogart said modestly, 'My home, Mr. Brown, I hope you'll pay me the honour of a short visit. Now let's get down there and you can sling that woman in a corner while we talk. There's a lot that you're going to tell me, Mr. Brown.'

Larry turned his head to see Rogart smiling at him over the barrel of the Luger. Angrily he turned away and moved down towards the house.

A few minutes slithering down the slope brought them to a barely marked drive-way that led them towards the house. There was a waist-high wall around the property and the drive passed through a pair of ancient iron gates that looked as though they stayed permanently open. The grounds inside were unattended and the sparse shrubbery overgrown with gorse. The house was festooned with ivy and the walls appeared to be constructed of black flint. There was a tiny porch over the front door, supported by a pair of grey stone pillars.

Larry waited with the girl in his arms while Rogart moved around him and mounted the two steps to the porch. The man used a large key to open the lock, feeling for the keyhole with both eyes on his captives. He pushed the door open

and pressed a light switch just inside.
Beyond him Larry saw a narrow hall,
paper peeling from the walls.

Rogart stepped back from the door
with a mock bow.

'Enter, Mr. Brown, welcome to my
humble abode.'

Larry climbed the steps and turned
sideways to manœouvre Linda's limp
form through the doorway. She had
closed her eyes and was half asleep in
his arms. The light fell on her white
face and she opened her lips. She stirred
vaguely but had no strength to do more
than glance around their surroundings.

Larry waited in the hall while Rogart
entered behind him. Larry wondered why
on earth the man chose to live alone in
this lost mausoleum deep in the lonely
highlands. The place had grim, unlived
in air.

'Well, Mr. Brown.' Rogart's voice was
harsh and threatening. 'Now you can tell
me all you know. All of it!'

The door slammed heavily behind him.

16

Rogart Regrets

Larry turned as the door closed behind them, Linda still in his arms.

'What the hell is this place?' he demanded angrily.

Rogart smiled amiably. 'I told you, it's my home. I bought it during the war for reasons of my own and have never found a buyer for it since. So I've kept it. The postal address is Lairg House, but the children in the nearest villages call it the hermit's, or crazy man's.'

'So you're a crazy hermit.'

Rogart remained unruffled. 'No, I'm not. But I get much more privacy by maintaining the rumours. You are really honoured, Mr. Brown. You're the first stranger to pass through that door for many years.'

Larry started to reply but Rogart cut him off by gesturing to a door on their

274

left. 'Take the girl in there,' he said. 'It's too draughty to talk in the hall.'

Larry opened the door with difficulty and kicked it wide. In the gloom he could just make out the shapes of a pair of large easy chairs facing an old-fashioned fireplace. He moved towards them and put Linda down gently as Rogart switched on the light. Then he turned round slowly. Apart from a small bare table there was no other furniture.

Rogart said cheerfully. 'My living-room. Please don't drop ash on the carpet.'

There was no carpet.

Larry said tightly, 'I'm beginning to think you must be mad.'

Rogart smiled. 'Not quite. But I am impatient to hear you start talking.'

'Why? What makes it so important to you?'

'I think you know that. If you found Konrad's haversack then you probably know what's in it. It couldn't have taken a lot of imagination to realize why I wanted it.'

'I haven't a clue what's in it. We never

had a chance to open it.'

Rogart laughed. 'Then why was it necessary to kill off the three men with you? And then try to cover up with a fake loss of memory story? You know, if you hadn't been so eager to get back to the mine I might have believed that yarn. You almost convinced me back at the hospital. Then when I read that you had broken out I realized I had been right the first time. A man with no memory would have no reason to run from the police.'

Larry scowled. 'Your story gave me a reason.'

'It hardly matters. Tell me what happened down there.'

Angrily Larry told him. With the haversack deep underwater there was little likelihood of the knowledge doing the man any good anyway. When he mentioned the rats Rogart frowned.

'So Marnoch's specimens were breeding in the old mine,' he mused. 'Crane said they were but I thought he was just bluffing to raise the price. The damned things were so dangerous that I had to go up to a thousand pounds to get him to go on with the job. I had to give him the gun too.' His eyes went hard and he added. 'The fool deserved to die if he did pull it on Lucas and the others like that. I don't suppose the daft idiot even thought of anything as simple as offering to take it up and removing what we wanted *en route*. They could have had the rest.'

'So Crane was going to murder us to earn the thousand pounds you had offered him. What made the pack so valuable to you?'

Rogart eyed him thoughtfully. 'So you really don't know. It seems that I owe you some apologies. I had you figured out all wrong. I was pretty sure that you must have found that pack and opened it. I forgot Crane's story about the rats in the old workings. As you know that gun you were holding when you were pulled up was the one I had given to Crane. I got a close enough look to recognize it. I deduced from that that Crane had tried to take the pack at gunpoint and that you had overpowered him and taken the gun. Then I assumed that you had realized the full value of the pack and shot all three of your companions to keep it, bringing down the shaft at the same time. Having assumed that much I took it for granted that you had conveniently lost your memory to avoid being questioned and meant to retrieve the haversack later. In fact I was expecting you to escape, and was quite pleased with myself when you did.'

Larry said curiously: 'How would all this intrigue have helped me? I should still have been hunted as a murderer.'

Rogart laughed. 'So what? The only murderers that have to worry are those that get caught. A bold man would have taken the risk. Your gamble was to keep the police at bay until you were fit to break out of that nursing home. And that was easy. They hadn't the slightest idea that there was anything of value down there and rated you a maniac. They quite believed in your loss of memory. A lot of homicidals kill in a blackout.' Rogart's smile grew broader. 'In fact, Mr. Brown, both the police and myself were perfectly satisfied with our different reconstructions of the crime. It seems we were both a little off track.'

Larry said wryly, 'Well, I'm glad I've convinced one of you that I'm speaking the truth. What puzzles me now is how you knew where to find me. The police were keeping my whereabouts a secret.'

A trace of amusement played in Rogart's green eyes. 'True, but our local police knew and it's easy enough to pump a man who trusts you. It only cost me a social evening in the local pub to find out. Even a policeman likes an off-duty drink.'

Linda said suddenly: 'I suppose it was you who tried to break into the nursing home two nights ago.'

'It was. I wanted to continue my talk with Mr. Brown, but I couldn't risk a disturbance when he got flustered. That and hiring Crane are the only risks I've had to take so far. Crane was a big risk to me, but I had to have someone with free access to the mine. There were brighter men I could have employed, but an intelligent person would have realized how to exploit the contents of Konrad's pack for much more than the miserable one thousand pounds I was offering. So, it had to be Crane.'

Larry asked bluntly, 'What is in that pack?'

Rogart chuckled. 'I'll give you a clue, Mr. Brown. The mysterious something in that haversack could make me a fortune — or hang me. It all depends into whose hands it falls.'

Larry glared at him for a moment. 'Then I sincerely hope it hangs you,' he said. 'Whatever it is.'

Rogart remained unruffled. 'I don't think it will. By the way, whereabouts in the mine is it?'

'It must be still near the shaft, where we dropped it.'

'Thank you, Mr. Brown. That's all I need to know. My only problem now is to reach it before the police do.'

Larry looked up. 'Reach it? How?'

'In diving kit. The same way that the police intend to. They broke into the old workings late this afternoon and then found they couldn't go further.

They decided then to send for a team of naval divers to go down and recover the bodies, if possible. However it'll take the best part of the day for them to travel up here, so they're not scheduled to go down until tomorrow. I intend to do down tonight?'

Larry leaned against the wall by the big fireplace. 'Where do you expect to get diving kit from?' he demanded.

'I've already got it. As you know, a lot of the lower galleries on the seaward side of the main shaft were flooded before you went down. It was quite possible that Konrad's haversack was somewhere along these. When Crane had thoroughly seached all the higher galleries I meant to take him underwater with me to go through the lower tunnels. I should have had to have gone down then. So you see, I'm one jump ahead of the police, I have my equipment all ready to use. As soon as night falls again I'm going to retrieve that haversack.'

'You'll freeze.' Larry told him. 'That water is near to zero, I should think. We almost froze by just wading half way.'

Rogart smiled again. 'I have the proper frogmen's rubber suits, Mr. Brown. I know all about the temperature of the water.'

Larry glared into the black barrel of the Luger in Rogart's hand. He was realizing now that he had made a big mistake in giving Rogart the location of the haversack. If the evidence were removed he was going to find it almost impossible to prove his story to the police. Then another, even grimmer thought hit him.

He asked, 'What happens to us?'

Rogart smiled faintly. 'I really haven't given that much thought yet, but I shall. It should be easy to work something out. After all, the girl is officially feared dead, everyone expects her corpse to turn up in a ditch somewhere. And of course you are a wanted murderer on the run. I might just strangle her and hand you over to the police. I should have to work all the angles out first though.'

Larry looked into the cold green eyes and knew that the man was quite callous enough to carry out his threat. Rogart would kill without a moment's hesitation if he thought it necessary. There was no pity in the cold green eyes. They were hard and brittle, like frosted green glass.

Linda said slowly, 'Why must you kill us?'

'Surely that is obvious. You know far too much.'

'We know nothing,' Larry snarled. 'Except that you want that mouldy haversack for some reason of your own.'

'Exactly, and that is too much. If you were to talk, the police would become very interested in that haversack. They might even succeed in getting hold of it. Then they could hang me. I just can't afford that risk.' He paused and then went on thoughtfully, 'That seems to rule out my first idea, doesn't it? The police just might investigate your ramblings if I hand you over to hang for Miss Denning's murder. It seems that, much as I regret it, I shall have to think of a way to eliminate you both. With convincing explanations of course.'

Rogart smiled calmly and slipped cautiously off the table. 'Don't worry about it. I'll think of something really satisfactory.' He made a slight motion with the gun. 'Now just turn around, Mr. Brown. Face the wall and forget all about it.'

'And get shot in the back? No, thank you. I'd rather stare you out when you pull that trigger. It might give you nightmares afterwards.'

'I doubt it,' Rogart answered mildly. 'But you really have nothing to fear at the moment. If I meant to shoot you now I'd let you face me and claim self-defence. If you were shot in the back I might have trouble explaining it to the police. So just turn around and face the wall.'

Larry glowered defiantly through the slit in his bandages, then turned slowly round to face the wall. He wasn't sure what Rogart intended and by the time the obvious occurred to him it was a little too late. He heard Rogart cross the room towards him and felt uneasy. Then the truth dawned as Rogart reversed the Luger and smashed downwards with the butt at his white bound head. Larry heard the swish of the gun as it swept through the air but before he could move, it exploded against the base of his skull.

His head snapped forwards to hit the wall and then his knees buckled from under him. He slid into an untidy heap in the fireplace.

Linda started to her feet, her face white.

Rogart calmly dropped the Luger in his pocket and turned towards her.

'I don't think I need that to handle you,' he observed. 'You may have spirit but you're too weak to have any fight.'

He chuckled softly and moved towards her.

17

The Long Wait

Larry was lying face down on a stone floor when he regained consciousness. A fiery pain was throbbing in his temples and there was a bitter taste in his mouth. He moaned painfully.

From somewhere near a voice said urgently: 'Larry!'

He groaned again through clenched teeth, and then slowly his mind began to function. He could feel his arms twisted up behind him, and realized that his wrists were lashed together. The bare stone beneath him was cold to his naked chest for his jacket was open. He was chilled all over. The very marrow in his bones seemed frozen.

'Larry? Larry, are you all right?'

The voice came from above him and he stirred weakly. He twisted his head to one side and saw a pair of trim ankles, streaked with mud, and some of his pain melted into hot anger as he saw a harsh grey rope biting into the soft flesh. He followed the neat line of her bare legs up to the knees, and then with an effort rolled over on his side. Linda was lashed into a chair with her arms behind its back. He was lying full length at her feet.

'Larry?' She was looking down at him, her shoulders pulled back by the restraining ropes. 'Larry, are you all right?'

He winced. 'About as all right as anyone else with an A-bomb going off where his head should be.'

She stared at him anxiously and he had to force a smile before she breathed a sigh of relief, her breasts thrusting hard at her blouse as she relaxed.

'You don't know how you worried me,' she faltered. 'You've been out for hours.'

'What happened then, after Rogart knocked me out?'

'He made me come down here. He put the gun in his pocket and said he didn't

need it to handle me. I was terrified,'
she shuddered. 'I thought he was going
to strangle me, like he said. But he only
tied me up. Then he went back and
brought you down here as well. He said
that knocking you out first was the safest
way with you. I think he was just a little
bit afraid that you were going to attack
him, despite his gun. I was too.'

Larry grimaced and the movement sent
another wave of dull pain pulsing through
his aching temples. Slowly he glanced
around.

They were in the centre of a large
cellar. To his left, behind Linda's chair,
was a narrow grating set high in the
wall. A stream of light flooded through
at a steep angle that told him that it
was somewhere near noon. Whether just
before or after he could not tell without
knowing whether they were on the east
or west side of the house. Some tufts of
grass grew against the grilled bars and
he realized that they marked the level
of the ground outside. Behind him on
the opposite side of the cellar a flight of
stone stairs led up to a very solid looking

door. The floor of the cellar was littered with junk that was just dimly visible in the small amount of light from the grill. The bare stone floor was thick with dust and it was clear that the cellar had not been used for some time, except by the spiders who had draped the corners with the grey-black curtains of their webs.

'Not very cheerful, is it?' Linda couldn't keep a little quiver out of her voice as she spoke. 'I just hate spiders.'

'I wish that was all we had to worry about.' He twisted himself around so that he could look up at her. 'How are you feeling after last night?'

'Better now. I've had several hours rest sitting here.'

'I'm glad of that. You were all in when you collapsed on the moors.'

'I know, I still haven't thanked you for carrying me. I think that green-eyed swine would have left me there otherwise. With a bullet in my back.'

'I got you into this, didn't I?'

She smiled down at him but before she could answer he rolled forwards suddenly and kissed her bare leg just above the biting ropes. He felt a tremble run through her at the gentle contact of his lips and lingered there before drawing back. The kiss had been an impulse but she accepted it without embarrassment.

For a long time after that they were both silent with their own thoughts. Thoughts that ran together on parallel paths. Thoughts that had nothing to do with their immediate fate.

Their dreams were cut sharply dead when the door behind them rattled and creaked open. Larry twisted on the floor as fresh light flooded into the gloomy cellar. He saw Rogart's tall gaunt shape standing at the top of the steps.

The man moved swiftly down towards them. A smile played about his mouth but he seemed slightly agitated.

'Good morning,' he greeted them formally. 'And how are my reluctant guests this bright and sunny morning?'

Larry thought that the bantering tone was a little forced and said sarcastically. 'Our consciences are clear anyway. How is yours?'

Rogart laughed at that. 'I mentally

strangled it the first time it bothered me. I never have any qualms now.' He stopped in front of them and prodded Larry gently with his toe. 'How's the head, Mr. Brown? Not too bad I trust. I should hate your last hours to be painful ones.'

Larry ignored the humour. 'What the hell do you want now?'

'Listen,' Rogart lifted a hand as if for silence. 'Listen and you should be able to guess.'

For a moment all three remained silent. There was no sound and Larry was just about to speak again when a high pitched howl split the distant stillness. It stopped the words in his throat and he remained listening until the howl echoed again. Then he realized what it was.

The police were combing the moors with dog teams.

Rogart said cheerfully. 'You didn't tell me that you crashed a police road block last night and then ran the police car into a field. You also didn't tell me that you broke into the office at the mine and stole some maps of the galleries and some headlamps. I had to learn all that from the radio. Those events have convinced the police that you are somewhere in the area. They found your abandoned car so they know that you must be afoot. And at the moment they're searching the moors for you with tracker dogs.' He laughed. 'It's just as well I took you in isn't it? Out there in the open you wouldn't stand a chance.'

Larry said tightly, 'It couldn't matter. I have nothing to fear from the police now.'

'Perhaps not, but I have. So I very much regret that I shall have to gag the pair of you before they get too close. Those dogs might cross our trail and lead them this way. And they could hear you through the grill if you started to shout.' He reached into his pocket and drew out a bundle of neatly folded handkerchiefs. 'Ladies first, Miss Denning. Open your mouth please. Don't worry, these are quite clean, fresh from the laundry.'

Linda clamped her lips together defiantly but Rogart's smile didn't even fade. He fitted one hand around her chin and dug his finger and thumb viciously into the back of her jaws near the joints, forcing them apart. She opened her mouth a little and gasped with the sudden pain. He stuffed a handkerchief swiftly between her teeth and catching hold of her head poked it into her mouth with his finger.

'Don't bite,' he warned amiably. 'It's unladylike.'

She choked and writhed against the ropes as he bound a second handkerchief around her mouth and knotted it behind her neck. She stopped struggling and glowered at him sullenly.

'Very effective,' applauded Rogart cheerily. 'Every mother-in-law should have one.' He turned to Larry. 'Now you, Mr. Brown. And don't force me to be cruel as I was with Miss Denning. It might burst the stitches in your cheeks and the blood would make a mess in my cellar.'

Larry said nothing and submitted, mentally fuming, to being gagged in the same fashion. There was no point in resisting for the man must eventually have his own way. Rogart knelt over him to tie the handkerchief, his green eyes slightly regretful. Larry had the feeling that the man would have preferred him to put up a fight and get hurt. Rogart liked putting on the ruthless manner and enjoyed a little hopeless competition.

Rogart finally straightened up. He was still grinning as he replaced the rest of the neatly folded handkerchiefs in his pocket.

'That should ensure that you stay quiet and peaceful,' he said. 'Now I can go up and prepare to welcome the stalwart guardians of the law when they reach my gates. They might expect to find you hiding in the outhouses but never in a million years will they guess that you're being held prisoners inside the house.'

Unable to speak, Larry merely scowled.

Rogart went on, 'It's a shame really that they'll go on to spend the rest of the day searching the moors and mountainsides for a maniac who isn't there. Still' — he brightened — 'it's a nice day for it.'

He turned and walked back up the stairs. At the top he glanced back once and then closed the heavy oak door behind him. They heard the grim rattling a second time as he turned the key in the lock.

There was nothing they could do then except listen as the howls of the searching dogs drew nearer. In his mind's eye Larry could picture the scene as the local police and their helpers scoured the hills and moorlands. The bloodhounds straining at the leash and nosing head down through the gorse and heather. The dogs were certain to lead them here if they once picked up their trail but it was unlikely that it would do them any good. Rogart had only to let them search the outbuildings and ensure them that no one could have got into the house and they would depart. They would have no reason to suspect the man. Rogart was the kind of man who could lie as easily and unconcernedly as other men told the truth.

Time passed but they had no way of keeping track of it. The yelping of the dogs were no longer distant now and they were converging fast on the house.

Larry picked out four distinct notes in the baying and decided that two pairs of dogs were being used. The sounds became loud and clear and above them he heard the shouts of men. The noise of the search closed in on the house and they heard the murmur of voices above them. The dogs yelped excitedly and he heard one voice raised in a loud and easily distinguishable curse out of the hub-bub.

Larry saw Linda's eyes staring at him over the top of her gag and looked desperately around the cellar. If only he could find some way to make a loud enough noise he might be able to attract attention. He began to roll clumsily across the stone floor towards the cluttered junk on the far side. Linda watched him go with worried eyes, straining at the ropes that held her to her chair.

Larry rolled up against a pile of old boards and props that leaned against the wall. It took him several moments to work his body round to the right position. He raised his bound legs for a swing, and in that moment the cellar door opened.

Rogart's voice snapped, 'Don't Mr. Brown. The same idea occurred to me half a minute ago. The search party are going through the outhouses now but if you try anything like that I'll make sure that both you and the girl are dead when they find you.'

Larry turned away to see Rogart standing in the cellar doorway, a kitchen knife gleamed in his hand.

'This is silent, Mr. Brown. Now roll back to the girl before I use it. And don't make a noise. I may as well hang for one crime as for another.'

Bitterly Larry started to roll back across the floor towards Linda. Without a pause Rogart slammed the door behind him and they heard him racing away. Rogart wanted to keep a watchful eye on the searchers in his grounds.

For another ten minutes or so they heard the sounds of the dogs and searchers moving about the grounds of Lairg House. Larry listened to them with a knot of anger tightening in his stomach. If he tried to kick anything over it would most certainly be heard first by Rogart who was probably watching from the doorway of the house. He could come down and knife them long before they had made enough noise to attract attention. And he was the kind who would. There was nothing they could do.

The sounds of the searchers began to fade and after a while there was only the mournful baying of the dogs. The animals howled in long-drawn wails, their voices whining like wind demons across the moors and through the nearer mountain crags.

Soon even the eerie howling was lost in the distance.

Larry lay patiently at Linda's feet, waiting for Rogart to return and remove the gags from their mouths. The disappointment as the searchers moved away died slowly, even though it had been a vain hope all along. He began to get stiff as he waited and wondered how Linda was faring above him. She seemed relaxed and still in her chair, as if realizing that anything she might do would be a waste of effort. The stream of light through the narrow grating in the wall mover further away until it vanished altogether leaving just a faint glow through the grill. That meant that the sun had moved directly over the building. The grating must be facing east and it would now be just after noon.

Another hour or two passed before Rogart finally came below again. He faced them with the usual cynical, slightly sadistic, smile.

'You know, you very nearly got yourself killed,' he told Larry. 'If you had started making a row I shouldn't have hesitated to use that knife. And that would have been a shame, because I've planned a much more satisfactory ending for you.'

He leaned downwards and unknotted the gag from Larry's mouth. Larry spat the second handkerchief out and spluttered a little before he could speak.

'Thanks. You're so kind and considerate.' He put all the sarcasm he could muster into the words.

Rogart was unimpressed. 'I pride myself in having a sense of humanity,' he commented. 'All condemned persons are allowed a few privileges. And as necessity forces me to deny you most of them, the least I can allow is a last conversation with your loved one for the next few hours.' He turned away and began to remove the gag from Linda's mouth.

Larry watched him angrily. The man was a mysterious mixture of the ruthless sadist and cynical comedian. It seemed impossible that two such wildly conflicting characteristics could be combined in the one man, yet they were. In the dangerous moments when there was some threat to himself Rogart was viciousness to the core. At other times nothing seemed to ruffle him.

Linda shook her head free of the gag but did not speak.

Rogart eyed her casually and remarked, 'What, no thanks? I thought you were the politest one of the two.'

Larry said suddenly, 'You just mentioned something about a condemned man's privileges. How about the traditional hearty breakfast for two. We're practically starving.'

Rogart laughed. 'That's what I meant

about being forced to deny them to you. You see, when the police find you they will find a desperate, starving, criminal who died trying to break into my house for food. It will spoil the whole impression if you're found with a good meal still in your stomach.'

'All right — just feed her.'

'That's impossible too. The kind of man you will appear to be would not have fed his hostage while he starved himself. Especially as he was soon to kill her. So she must appear to be empty-bellied as well. If she were found to have just enjoyed a good meal it would strike that one strange note that just might make a smart detective wonder. That's the way some of our best murderers in past years have ended on the gallows. They forgot that one little flaw in their plans that made a smart dectective begin to wonder.' Rogart laughed softly. 'However you can leave all the sordid little details to me. I'll leave you alone now to pay your last respects to each other. You have until nightfall. In your own company it shouldn't be a long wait. You must have plenty to talk about while you pass the time.'

His green eyes were dancing with humour as he went out.

The long wait after he had gone passed slowly. They spent it in trying to puzzle out the meaning behind Rogart's deliberately vague references to Konrad's haversack. Who was Konrad? Or rather who had he been? And how could the contents of his rotting haversack mean either death or a fortune? Rogart had said it could hang him if it fell into another's hands, or at least had implied that much. But how? The riddle seemed insoluble and they began to wonder whether there was an answer at all. It would just amuse Rogart's twisted sense of humour to set them a crazy problem that meant nothing.

The time dragged and they became stiff and sore in their bonds. There was no feeling left in their wrists and ankles where the ropes cut in. The pains of hunger began to gnaw at their empty stomachs. Their mouths dried up with thirst and they talked less. It became gloomier than ever as the sun set and the light from the grill faded. In time they could only make out the outline of each other and the faint grey streaks that marked the location of the grill.

It was pitch dark when Rogart returned.

He switched on a light just inside the cellar door and the sudden light blinded them. By the time they could see again he had descended the steps and stood over them, smiling.

The kitchen knife gleamed in his hand.

He said calmly, 'Well, this is it. Night has fallen and the dirty work can commence.'

Larry said tightly, 'What kind of dirty work?'

'Your timely exit from this world, Mr. Brown. During the day I've had plenty of time to work out the details. I've kept it simple because simple plans are usually the best. First I intend to strangle Miss Denning and dump her body on the moors. Then I shall come back, shoot you, Mr. Brown, and arrange your corpse in a suitable position in my garden. The overall impression gained by the police will be of a desperate and starving maniac disposing of his hostage and then attempting to break into the home of an honest house-holder in an effort to steal food, the aforesaid honest house-holder having shot you dead in defence of his property.' He smiled: 'Neat isn't it, Mr. Brown?'

He received no answer and turned to Linda. 'I hope you won't mind Miss Denning but I hardly feel inclined to hump your body over the moors. So perhaps you'll allow me to walk you to your last resting place.'

He rolled Larry calmly out of the way with his foot and proceeded to cut her free with the kitchen knife.

18

A Bid for Freedom

The blade of the kitchen knife was razor-sharp and sliced easily through the thick cords that bound Linda's ankles. The cords dropped away leaving deep, ribbed, grooves in the white flesh. Larry watched helplessly as Rogart moved round the chair to cut her arms free. At that moment he was cursing himself more than ever before for allowing her to share his troubles.

Rogart stood to one side as Linda brought her hands slowly from behind the chair and looked at the ugly rope marks on her wrists. She began to rub them gently with each palm in turn and winced when she tried to flex her fingers.

Rogart laughed softly. 'Take a little time, Miss Denning, and get that circulation going again. You've got quite a long walk ahead of you.'

Larry strained frantically at the ropes, feeling them bite viciously into his wrists. It was useless.

Rogart went on: 'As soon as I have disposed of you two, I shall use a frogman's suit to go down after Konrad's pack. Just think, within a few months time I shall probably be one of the richest men in England.' He smiled and eyed Linda who was still tentatively massaging her wrists. 'Forget your hands, Miss Denning, you won't need those any more. Try getting some life into your feet. Then we can start walking.'

Larry exerted all his remaining strength in one last agonizing effort to snap his bonds, and failed.

Linda stood up slowly and gritted her teeth as her weight came on to her feet. She had to hold the chair for support and stood there for several seconds, trying to maintain her balance.

Rogart fingered the edge of the kitchen knife almost thoughtfully. 'Rub your ankles,' he ordered her. 'You'll be all right.'

Linda kept one hand on the chair and used the other to massage around the vicious grooves where the ropes had cut in. After a minute or so she let go of the chair altogether and stooped so that she could use both hands, rubbing each ankle in turn. Rogart watched as she tried to work her blood into circulation. She didn't look up. He smiled confidently to himself.

Linda felt little streaks of fire begin to shoot through her ankles. Sharp pains that tingled and burned all the way down to her toes. She bit her lip to hold back a little cry and began to put more pressure into her massaging. The fiercer pain of her sore flesh helped to drown the fire of her slowly moving bloodstream. Then suddenly she cracked her elbow on the chair.

She hadn't realized that she was still that close to the chair and impulse and the raw instinct for survival caused her to act instantaneously. She saw her chance in the chair and grabbed it without thought. She caught the nearest chair leg in one hand and straightened up swiftly, putting all her strength into one savage upward swing of the chair.

The chair came up and across in a fast arc that took the over-confident Rogart completely unawares. The seat smashed into the side of his face with a vicious smack, sending him reeling across the cellar. Linda almost fell over as his knife clattered to the stone floor, then she drew the chair back and used both hands to hurl it across the cellar at the staggering killer. It hit Rogart smack in the pit of the stomach and knocked him flying to the ground.

Linda collapsed to her knees with the force of her throw and then scurried in a desperate crawl towards the knife that lay glinting on the floor several yards away. She reached it and yelled to Larry to roll over as she turned back. Larry rolled on to his face and seconds later felt the pull of the ropes as she slashed the knife through them. His wrists fell apart and with another swift stroke she freed his ankles. Larry pushed himself clumsily to his knees.

Across the floor Rogart shook his head

dazedly as he watched the girl cut the faceless man free. He lurched to his feet with his head still ringing from the first blow with the chair. As Larry gained his feet and charged him in a staggering run he thrust one hand into his pocket and closed his fingers round the cold butt of his Luger pistol. The mummified face with savage burning eyes was almost upon him when he wrenched the gun free.

Larry saw Rogart's hand coming out of his pocket and with it the black gleam of the Luger. Desperately he hurled himself forward, his arms closing round the other's hips and clamping his gun hand to his side. Somehow Rogart stayed up straight beating down with his free fist at the top of Larry's bandaged skull. Larry felt the pounding fist rocking his head and gritted his teeth as he hung on. If he let go he would only fall for his legs were too stiff to do anything but trail limply behind him. And once he let go of Rogart's gun hand the other could shoot.

Rogart swore and then risked being

knocked off balance by bringing his knee up hard into Larry's chest. Larry jerked back on his knees, his hold already slipping. Then Rogart brought his knee up again, hard and vicious and full into Larry's bandaged face.

Larry arched over backwards with a scream of pain as the stitches split open in his cheek. He felt a surge of blood seep out into the white dressings and it seemed that his whole face had opened up. He hit the stone floor with his legs still bent beneath him and twisted in a haze of agony.

Rogart stepped back panting and lifted the Luger.

Linda still held the kitchen knife. Larry's scream stirred a mixed response of rage and heart-felt pain within her breast. She was already moving forward as Rogart raised the gun and she brought the knife down on his wrist with a wild chopping blow. Rogart yelled as the keen blade bit into his flesh, cutting deep to the bone. Blood spurted in a bright red fountain and swiftly drenched the back of his hand. The Luger shot from his sharply splayed fingers and hit the ground.

Larry, blood already showing on his white swathed features, rolled towards the fallen gun. Rogart backed up in pain, clutching at his cut wrist, while Linda recoiled in sudden horror as she saw the blood smearing the silver blade of her knife.

Larry's hand closed over the gun. He felt the hard squared butt in his palm and with it a sense of power.

Rogart hesitated but Larry was just too far away for him to risk a spring. He turned and raced for the steps that led out of the cellar.

Larry rolled up on to his left elbow and aimed at Rogart's fast moving back. He lost two or three seconds in fumbling his finger through the trigger guard and fired. The bark of the gun filled the cellar and the weapon bucked slightly in his hand. Rogart reached the door as the bullet ricocheted off the wall half a yard from his head. Before Larry could fire again he was out of the cellar and had slammed the heavy door behind him. They heard

311

the rattle as he paused to turn the key in the lock.

Larry lowered the gun, cursing his rotten aim until the pain from his split face made him faint. Linda threw the blood-stained kitchen knife into a corner and knelt over him. An area of red as large as a man's fist stained the bandages about his cheek. He was breathing harshly and the touch of her hands brought him round. He felt sick and weak but a burning sense of urgency forced him not to slip back again.

'Larry, Larry are you all right?' She was on her knees with his head cradled in her lap, her eyes filled with fear.

He struggled up and she helped him into a sitting position. Shuffling close behind him to support his head on her shoulder.

'I — I'm okay.' The lie was half strangled through his tight clenched teeth.

He got to his feet, swaying like a ship's mast in a gale. His body seemed drained of energy and his face hurt like fury. Linda had to hold him to prevent him from falling.

It took him several minutes to become capable of standing upright without help. The long hours of waiting, bound hand and foot, had cramped up his muscles into a solid mass. He had not even had the few minutes that Linda had taken to get the blood circulating a little before she acted. He massaged his wrists slowly as his mind began to function again. The first thing he thought of was Linda.

He took her arm feverishly. 'Linda, you didn't get hurt did you?'

She shook her head weakly. 'No, I felt a little sick when I cut him with the knife, that's all. It wasn't the blood, I'm used to that. It was just the fact that I had done it. I'm not sorry, but I couldn't help that queasy feeling all the same.'

Larry found he could think more clearly now. The pain in his face still raged but one part of his mind was working coldly and calmly, completely unaffected. It told him he had to catch up with Rogart.

He gasped weakly, 'Let's get ourselves fit again, then we can think about getting out.'

Linda nodded in agreement and they

spent a painful five minutes in massaging their wrists and ankles until the blood was running freely. At the finish their limbs still tingled with pain but at least they could walk without limping.

Linda said grimly, 'What now?'

Larry ignored the throbbing of his injured face. 'Right now we've got to get after Rogart. He'll make for the mine. He must do. If he gets there and removes that haversack, I've had it. Without that I've nothing to prove a motive either for Crane to have attacked my party down the mine, nor for Rogart to have kept us here all day. It'll be our word against his and the convictions of the police. I don't think there's a single hope that the police would believe our version.'

He grinned and hooking one arm about her waist he led her up the stone stairs to the door. Aiming Rogart's Luger point-blank at the lock he fired. Splinters flew from the woodwork and even above the roar of the gun they heard the rending of twisted metal as the bullet ploughed through the mechanism. Larry fired again and kicked the door wide open.

They found themselves facing the narrow hall with the front door at the far end. Four doors led off from the hall but all were closed. To their right the hall continued for another few yards behind them and ended against yet another door. Larry stood there warily, keeping Linda back with his free hand and wondering which room Rogart had entered.

The clue to Rogart's whereabouts reached them suddenly in the note of a car engine starting up outside. Larry sprinted down the hall and then abruptly hesitated at the door. Rogart had had several minutes in which to get away while they had been recovering themselves in the cellar. Why had he waited until he heard them shoot their way out before starting up his car? Cautiously Larry waved Linda back. When he yanked the door open he kept behind it.

The bark of an automatic made him press himself even more against the wall as Rogart ripped off three fast shots through the open doorway.

Through the thin slit where the door hinged on to the post Larry saw Rogart leaning out of the front window of a Vauxhall. Rogart had expected him to come rushing blindly out of the door when he heard the engine but now that his surprise attack had failed he let in his clutch and roared away. Larry sprang out into the open and sent two shots into the Vauxhall as it careered down the drive. The car swerved crazily as Rogart took avoiding action and then jolted through the open gates and down the rough track.

Larry held his fire and swore.

Linda came up behind him as the Vauxhall disappeared into the night. There was no mist but the sky was black with clouds again and it didn't take many minutes for the darkness to swallow the car. Soon even the sound of the engine was dying.

Linda said tightly, 'I never thought he'd have another gun.'

'Neither did I,' Larry thrust the Luger into his pocket as he spoke. 'But he had plenty of time to gather up all he needed before we came out of the cellar.' He turned away bitterly and stared back up the hall.

'The telephone!' Linda ejaculated suddenly. 'The police might stop him before he reaches the mine, or at least catch him with the evidence on him as he leaves.'

Without a word Larry ran back into the house with Linda at his heels. He couldn't remember seeing any telephone in the room where Rogart had questioned them and deliberately passed it by. The two rooms on the left of the hall were empty apart from dust and dirt. In the second room on the right they found a desk and bookcase and the few bare necessities for a study. On the desk was a telephone.

Larry grabbed it and dialled treble nine. He stopped with his finger still on the dial as Linda bitterly held up the cut ends of the wires. Angrily he slammed down the receiver. Rogart forgot nothing.

'Come on,' he said grimly. 'We'll look around outside. There might be a push bike or something we can use. Anything that'll be faster than following him to the mine on foot.'

She followed on his heels as he ran back through the hall and into the grounds. The tyre tracks of Rogart's car led them round the side of the house to the garage but it was empty apart from spares and tools. Beside it was a wood shed but there were no bicycles. Further along was another low shed and they ran towards it as a last resort. It was locked.

Larry pulled the Luger from his pocket and thrust the barrel under the chain. There was no need to waste a bullet for a sharp wrench tore the staples holding the lock and chain from the rotten wood. Larry pocketed his gun and wrenched the door open. In the gloom they could just make out the bonnet of an ancient van.

Larry hesitated then plunged into the shed. He found the door handle and jerked it open. Swinging inside he fumbled for the controls. His heart was beating strangely fast and he began to pray that the old van would go. Linda appeared in the doorway beside him and a match suddenly flared in her hand.

'Good girl,' he whispered, and felt his hopes rise as he saw the key sticking out of the ignition. He twisted it but it wouldn't turn. He twisted harder and then gave it an angry wrench. The dashboard light glowed palely and he felt the thrill of success. He pulled open the choke and jerked the starter. There was no response. He tried half a dozen times before borrowing the last of Linda's matches to search for the starting handle. He found it almost under his feet.

For several minutes he swung the handle, feeling it kick savagely in his hand. He began to sweat and for a moment even the dull throbbing of his blood-stained face was forgotten. Then abruptly the engine fired, spluttered, and then died. Larry smiled at the sound and redoubled his efforts with the starting handle. The engine spluttered twice more before he finally got it going.

He jumped back inside and heard the gears grate as he put the van into first. He let in the clutch and there was a thunderous crashing from behind that told him that the van had been supporting a pile of junk. The stuff clattered down as he drove the van into the open and then Linda was swinging into the opposite side. There was no seat there and she squatted on her heels as he drove back to the front of the house. There he stopped.

'Larry, what now?' She caught his shoulder as he tried to get out.

He glanced back, his eyes grim. 'Rogart said he meant to take Crane with him — remember? That means he must have a spare suit. I'm going to follow him all the way.'

He ran back to the house, leaving the engine running, after a second or two Linda followed him.

They made straight for the far door beyond the cellar which opened, as Larry had suspected, on to the stairway to the upper storey. The old stairway smelt strongly of damp and decay, and the boards creaked noisily as they ran upwards.

A small passage at the top of the landing led into five different rooms. They found what they were looking for in the third room they tried. A small table near the wall was littered with maps of the old mine workings, many of the tunnels shaded red to show that they had been searched. On the opposite wall hung two complete frogman outfits and all the equipment needed for spear fishing. There was a pile of fishing rods and tackle as well as two sporting shotguns, so it seemed that Rogart was quite a sportsman.

Quickly Larry took down one of the rubber suits and flippers. He took a mask and oxygen bottles and then spent valuable minutes hunting for a rubberized torch. He heaved a sigh of relief as he found one, it would be essential in the flooded galleries.

Linda said abruptly, 'Are you ready?' She had gathered up the second suit and equipment in her arms.

His mouth tightened. 'You can drop those. This time I'm going alone.'

'Oh, no you don't, we're in this together — remember? I have done aqualung swimming.'

Larry hesitated and then realized that

every delay gave Rogart a larger start. And he could always argue with her in the van.

'Get going then,' he said curtly.

She left the room smiling as he took the spear-gun down from the wall. He was thinking of the rats as he took it but then he saw that there were now two empty racks, both identical. Rogart must have had the same idea and taken a gun as well.

A new and chilling thought struck him as he followed Linda out of Lairg House. Those vicious barbed spears would be equally effective against a man.

19

Back to the Mine

Linda watched the grim outline of Lairg House merge into the gloom as the commandeered van jolted wildly along the rough track back to the main road. Then slowly she turned to face Larry. His hands were clenched fast on the wheel and his foot was flat down. The large red stain on his cheek gave a horrific touch to his muffled features, and even she could hardly suppress a shiver. She knew he ought to have his face attended to as soon as possible, but knew too that he would never stop for that now. He wanted Rogart. And he meant to get him.

Larry was unaware of her thoughts, for he was busy with his own, concentrating on the track ahead that showed up as two wide furrows in the grass. The van was practically rupturing itself to keep up to a wavering forty-five. Larry swore at the lack of speed, but it probably saved their lives. If he had been driving anything faster he would have turned it over on the bumpy ground.

His bleeding face was a nagging pain that drove him on and on, but another spur goaded him even more than that.

Rogart had threatened Linda.

Rogart had to pay.

The track swerved left and Larry had to brake hard as they came up to the main road. The brake drums screamed and the wheels spun in the mud and grass before they slithered out on to the tarmac. The tyres bit again on the roadway but still the front wheels bounced on the opposite verge before the car skidded to a halt.

Larry hesitated before Linda said confidently: 'Left.'

He reversed the van and swung left. He recalled that when Rogart had marched them away from the mine the night before they had turned left away from the track and the sea. To turn left again now that they were coming from the opposite direction must bring them back to where that track met the road.

He got the straining van up to fifty as their headlights cut through the night. Over on their right he could just make out the outlines of the mountains, they towered up as black and forbidding as ever. Grimly he kept his eyes fixed on the right-hand side of the road, searching for the rough track that would take them up to the McArnot mine. When he saw it he was going too fast to stop and had to reverse back towards it for almost twenty yards. He pulled the wheel round and headed the van in the new direction before going up through his gears and stamping hard on the accelerator.

There was no conversation as they drove. Linda was too busy maintaining her balance and hanging on, while Larry had to keep his eyes fixed on the way ahead. He crouched over the wheel which seemed determined to jump from his grasp. While he fought one separate and distinct corner of his mind was focused coldly and clearly on a mental image of Rogart.

They still knew very little about the

man. He was callous, he had a warped sense of humour and he needed Konrad's haversack, but that was all they knew. Odd snatches of Rogart's conversation kept returning to Larry's mind and then suddenly two of them clicked together.

When he had talked of Konrad Rogart had said: 'He died of natural causes, natural for those times anyway.' And later in the cellar he had told them, 'I might as well be hung for one crime as another.' He hadn't said one murder or another, he had said one crime. And the only other hanging crime in England was treason. Perhaps Rogart did not know that the death penalty did not apply during peacetime. Larry thought of that reference to Konrad again. In what times could an unnatural death be considered natural? The answer was obvious, wartime. Thousands had died violently during the two great wars, their deaths had been natural enough for their times. Larry felt instinctively that he was on the right track. Konrad was a German sounding name. Sometime during the war Rogart had conspired with a man named Konrad to commit treason. And the contents of Konrad's haversack would prove it.

There were only three questions left.

How had the haversack become lost in the old mine?

Why was Rogart only now concerned with it, sixteen years after the war had ended?

And how could the proof of his guilt possibly make him a fortune if he reached it first?

Larry wanted to talk his theory over with Linda but there was no time. Already he could smell salt on the wind and hear the roar of the sea. They were following the coast and would soon be near the mine. And he had to catch Rogart before he moved that haversack. Everything hinged on that.

Linda said quietly, 'Ease up, Larry, we don't want to go over the edge.'

He realized that they were racing along the cliff edge with the steep sloping barrier of rock falling down to where the sea swirled against it far below. If they skidded off the track nothing could prevent them from sailing out into space and then diving into the white froth where land and sea clashed together. Reluctantly he eased his foot off the pedal. The van dropped speed by another five miles.

Abruptly the track swung right and they recognized the point where they had crossed it the night before. As they swung away from the cliff edge Larry trod down hard again and sent the van leaping forward. High up ahead they could see the hoist above the pit-shaft and the roof tops of the mine buildings. The slope was stiff and the van made frantic noises as it slowed up. Larry was forced to change down and then down again as the climb grew steeper. Before he reached the top the van was struggling sluggishly in bottom.

They came over the crown of the hill and found themselves facing the comparatively flat area where the pithead had been built. Drawn up in the centre of the buildings in front of the hoist shed was a sleek new car. It glinted brightly in the light of the van's headlamps. Larry recognized it as Rogart's Vauxhall.

He trod on the pedal and roared the van towards it, still in bottom gear. He braked opposite and then stiffened in alarm. Ahead of him lay the body of a man in the blue uniform of a policeman.

He licked his lips and then shut off the engine and climbed stiffly out. He brought the Luger out of his pocket as he stepped down and glanced around tensely. Rogart just might be waiting for him. He hesitated for long moments while Linda waited in the van. Then he reached in to switch off the van's headlights and walked over to the body. He didn't intend to be caught in the glare.

He looked down at the corpse, just as Linda came up beside him. He felt her shudder as she stood close. There was blood beneath the man showing where he had been shot in the stomach. The back of his head had also been shot away while he lay there. Rogart was taking no chances. The man might have survived the stomach wound to identify him, so the second shot had made sure.

Linda said tightly, 'Over there.'

Larry followed her pointing finger towards the lighted hut where the guards had sheltered the previous night. The light from the open doorway showed another crumpled figure lying before it. The figure wore ordinary clothes and must have been the watchman.

They didn't go over. Rogart would have made sure the man was dead before he left. Exactly the same as he had done with the constable. There was no other body so they assumed that the watch had been cut to two. No doubt the police were certain that they would not be back a second time.

Larry said grimly, 'Let's get after him.' He thrust the Luger back into his pocket, certain that if Rogart were around he would have been shot at by that time. He went to the back of the van and wrenched the doors open, forcibly snapping the string.

Linda said tightly, 'There might be a 'phone in that hut. Why not call the police and leave it to them.'

330

Larry pulled out a set of oxygen bottles and harness and put them on. It was going to be the easiest way of carrying them. He said, 'That's a good idea. You telephone and wait for them while I go on after him. You can explain things when they get here.'

She hauled out the second pair of bottles defiantly. 'I didn't mean that, and you know it. It won't take a couple of seconds to call them before we go into the mine. You're not going alone.'

'Oh, yes I am.' He fitted the face plate over his head. 'This time I'm not taking you. Rogart's a killer.'

'You've no choice, Larry darling. If you leave me I shall only follow you.' She buckled the harness and began to pile all the rest of the gear, suits, flippers and her mask into her grey coat.

'Linda, be reasonable, I don't want you down there. Can't you see that. I might not come back. In fact it's ten to one that either Rogart or I will die down there within the next hour. I don't want you killed as well.'

'I know, but you're not going alone.'

She picked up the coat full of gear by the corners and slung it over her shoulder. 'You go first with the torch.'

'Linda for the last time — '

The sudden howl of a dog cut him short.

They froze and then heard it again. The deep baying they had heard earlier that day. The searchers were still combing the moors. The first dog howled again and they realized that the search was closing in fast. Rogart's gunshots when he killed the guards must have carried a long way.

Linda said swiftly, 'No need to call them, they're nearly here.' She turned and ran for the hoist shed with the bundle of diving gear over her shoulder.

Larry hesitated, then he grabbed the spear-gun from the back of the van and followed her. Rogart was his personal enemy now and he was determined to settle the score before the police caught up with them.

The door to the hoist shed swung open and Larry saw a broken lock dangling from a chain. It seemed that after last night the mine company had decided to lock up their property. Only Rogart with a gun had no respect for locks or property. No more than he had for human life.

The hounds were baying closer behind them as they hurried inside and Larry switched on his torch. Swiftly he led the way to the emergency ladder and swung over the guard rails. He helped Linda over and then handed her the torch in exchange for the bundle of diving gear.

'I'm going first,' he said flatly. 'You shine the torch down for me.'

She didn't argue. Hurriedly he swung into the shaft, holding both the bundle and the spear-gun in his left hand. He let his right hand slide jerkily down the side of the ladder as he started to climb down. Linda swung on to the ladder above him. She held the torch down at arm's length to light his way.

As fast as they dared they began the descent.

The black shaft of the mine swallowed them up and soon the sound of the distant hounds died away. Larry forgot them immediately. His thoughts concentrated around the tall, gaunt Rogart. The killer had to be somewhere below them in the mine and the murdered bodies of the constable and the watchman proved the quality of the man with whom they were dealing. Rogart was viciousness to the core.

They would have to move warily.

Linda's mind held only one thought. Either Rogart or Larry had to die down there in the flooded galleries. She knew that that was the only way the coming clash could end.

And she was afraid.

Afraid for Larry because he lacked the merciless cruelty that was going to be so much to Rogart's advantage.

20

Underwater

The weight of the diving gear on his back threatened to tear Larry off the ladder as they descended further underground. Climbing with one hand had been easy enough at the start but as they progressed the strain made it increasingly harder. The muscles of his right arm began to ache angrily and the harness of the twin oxygen bottles pulled at his shoulders. His left arm began to ache too from being continually bent up over his shoulder to hold the bundle of gear. Long before they passed the first hundred feet he would willingly have jettisoned that bundle. Only without it he might not catch up with Rogart. And Rogart had to be caught.

Above him Linda was labouring with equal weariness. The bottles on her back had trebled in weight since they first swung into the shaft, and even the torch was becoming heavy. Once she closed her eyes and climbed blind but the resulting wave of dizziness almost threw her off the ladder. She began to think of food and realized that her stomach was actually aching with emptiness. Neither of them had eaten since those few sandwiches in the car two nights ago. She thought that the walls of her stomach must eventually cave inwards from lack of food. It was a strange thought but with it came a colder one. Larry must be weak with hunger too. That would be yet another card against him when he met up with the killer who lurked somewhere in the old galleries below them.

They passed the one hundred and fifty foot level without a pause. They badly needed a rest there but neither gave a thought to stopping. Rogart already had far too good a start. That last fifty feet to the bottom level was sheer torture for both of them. A fit man or woman would have made the climb with no worse effects than heaving lungs and a slightly faster heartbeat. But this was now the third night since they had left the nursing home and both Larry and Linda had been continually expending energy all the time. As soon as they gained a chance to build up any reservoir of strength, a new effort had drained it away. Apart from short rests on the train north and uncomfortable cat naps in Rogart's cellar they had had no sleep, and now they were almost as tired as they were hungry.

Only the burning desire to settle with Rogart kept Larry going now. He had forgotten the police and the haversack that might prove his story to them. Only Rogart mattered now. Rogart who had threatened Linda with death. Rogart who had to pay.

And Linda followed because she had to see him through. She couldn't let him climb alone to the final rendezvous with a killer in the depths of the old mine.

Larry reached the last rung and stepped down on to the uneven floor of the mine with a sigh of relief. He dropped his bundle to the ground and then remembered that Rogart might be nearby. His hand went to the Luger in his pocket and he stared uneasily into the darkness. Then commonsense returned and he relaxed. If Rogart was waiting in ambush he would have fired the moment they swung into view, not let them get off the ladder where they would have a chance. Rogart was probably swimming through the flooded galleries by now.

He turned to help Linda and lifted her down the last few rungs. She leaned against him heavily and smiled, her teeth were very white against her black-smudged face.

'Are you fit to go on?' he asked.

'Sure I'm fit.' She massaged her aching arm and winced slightly. She added: 'I'm fit as I shall ever be anyway.'

'All right then, we'll get going.' He picked up the bundle of gear and the spear-gun and threw them over his shoulder. With his right hand he again pulled the Luger out of his pocket. What with rats and Rogart it would be as well to have it ready.

Linda rearranged the harness of the oxygen bottles over her shoulders and shone the torch down the silent tunnel that they had walked the previous night. Together they walked down between the shiny steel rails that carried the coal trucks into the blackness.

It was an eerie feeling to be back down the mine again, two hundred feet under the ground. And there was a different atmosphere invading the silent tunnels. Last night they had walked in doubt, not knowing what they were going to find, or what to expect. Then the mine had exuded an air of mystery, a grim warning of unknown dangers. Now they knew what to expect and the mine held a sense of foreboding, a cold and solemn caution against impending death.

It made Linda shiver slightly as she walked.

There was no sound in the mine except their own footsteps. Larry walked with ears alert, realizing the full gravity of the risks they were taking. Rogart had only to wait in one of the branching tunnels until he saw their light coming towards him. He could let them get within point-blank range before he fired and they wouldn't stand a chance. The thought made Larry lick his dried lips but he went on. Somehow he was sure Rogart wouldn't be waiting in ambush yet. He needed that haversack too badly. That was where he and Rogart would meet — over the haversack.

They turned up the branching tunnel they had followed before, walking swiftly through the mine. There was no time for delay now. If Rogart should achieve his aims before they met then the man's next thought would be to lay in wait for them. That was if the man had remembered the van and realized that they had a way of following him. If he hadn't remembered that then his first thought would be to get clear of the mine before the two bodies were found at the pithead. In which case it would all depend on who saw the other's light first. Either way Larry wanted to catch up with the killer before he started tampering with the evidence that lay beneath the flooded galleries. If that was removed it was still possible that Larry would hang for the killing of Lucas and the other two men who had been with him in that first descent to the old galleries.

They reached the third left turn and hurried up the new direction towards the entry into the old workings that the police had had unblocked. Larry was beginning to realize just how much the odds were in Rogart's favour. If he and Linda died in the mine Rogart had only to hide the girl's body up one of the flooded tunnels and then transfer the blame for the two murders above. The police already considered Larry a homicidal maniac, and they would quite willingly accept that he had shot the two men above. All Rogart needed then was the ingenuity to explain away his own presence in the mine. Of course if he got clear without being seen he would not even have that worry. He could simply leave his gun in Larry's hand and allow the police to draw their own conclusions. Larry realized that unless he triumphed in the coming clash, Rogart could get away scot free. The thought served to harden his determination into grim resolve. Rogart had to be stopped.

They passed through the section of the tunnel that had been cleared and found themselves again in the narrow, crumbling tunnel into the old workings. The smell of rot and decay hit their nostrils again and Larry felt Linda press close against him as they walked. She kept her free hand on his arm now and when he looked at her he saw that her face was paler than ever, though her lips were still set firm. He felt fear twist and squirm in his empty stomach and wished that she were anywhere but here. If only she had stayed on the surface it would have been better. His mind would have been easier if she were safe and that feeling of dread would not be worming into his belly. If only he could have made her stay out of this. If only she had not insisted on following if he left her behind. It was better to have her with him than following alone in the darkness.

Linda sensed something of his thoughts and squeezed his arm in her fingers. She gave him a faint smile and received a vague twist of the lips in return. She knew he still didn't want her along, but knew too his chances would be lessened without her. Alone he would fight with an easier mind, but with her beside him he would have that much more incentive to win. The danger to her would be a spur to goad him into the same killing mood as his enemy, and just might tip the scales in his favour. He loved her, and he would fight with the last-ditch savagery of a jungle cat to defend her.

And she loved him enough to throw her life on the scales with his, just to give him that slightly better chance.

They moved on through the narrow confines of the old gallery until the black gleam of the sea glinted in the light of the torch. Linda stiffened and her hand closed tighter about Larry's arm. He lowered the bundle of diving equipment to the ground and stared down the tunnel, the Luger in his hand pointing across the black waters. He knew now that Rogart had to be somewhere under the surface of that black sea. The man had not had time to complete his business and get out of the mine before they entered. And the fact that they had not passed him meant that he must still be underwater.

Linda wet her lips with her tongue as he turned to face her. He said grimly:

'I'm going on after him. I'll take the spear-gun but leave you the Luger. If I come back I'll shout and let you know the moment I break water. If the man who comes up doesn't do that you'll know it must be Rogart. Don't take any chances — shoot him.'

She made one final effort to stop him rushing into that final clash. She said quietly: 'Why don't we both just wait here for him? We can cover him with the gun when he comes up.'

'No,' Larry's tone was sharp. 'If he moves that haversack we may never find it again in that flooded maze. Without that the police might still believe his story against ours.'

'It will be two against one.'

'Yes, but the police still consider me a killer, and you wouldn't be the first girl to perjure herself for a man she loved. The police would still have their doubts, and Rogart's story will be so much more plausible.'

She knew he was right. She said simply, 'Let's go then.' She shrugged her shoulders out of the harness and set the oxygen bottles on the ground before sorting out one of the rubber suits from the mound of equipment they had carried in her grey coat. She was ignoring completely his suggestion that she should wait behind.

Larry said angrily, 'I'm going alone, Linda.'

She unzipped her skirt and wriggled it down over her hips. 'Are you going to turn your back while I change into this frogman's suit or not?'

'Linda, I — '

She stepped out of the skirt and came closer to him. 'Larry, if we both go, our chances are higher. When we meet up with Rogart he'll have two of us to watch. If I can only distract his attention from you for a couple of minutes it might be enough. And I'm coming with you, how ever much you argue.' She kissed him lightly and added, 'And really, darling, I don't mind you watching. When we're on our honeymoon this will all be old stuff anyway.' She turned her back on him and began to struggle into the tight fitting rubber suit.

Larry watched her helplessly, knowing that she wouldn't stay behind. He moved over to help her pull the suit on and then held her tightly against him, hungrily grinding his lips against her mouth. There was nothing tender in that embrace for he knew that this might be the last time he would ever hold her. He kissed her fiercely and she answered with the same savage desire. The kiss made Larry's lacerated cheek throb in fury as they strove against one another, neither willing to relax and draw back. Their bodies merged in violent contact until the hunger died and they released each other — weak and trembling.

Larry drew a mouthful of breath and said simply, 'Let's go — together.'

She smiled and gave him a hand with his rubber suit after he had pulled off his outer clothing. The thick rubber fitted closely and they were sure that it would keep out a good bit of the cold. However they still intended to keep their time underwater as short as possible. They still remembered their last trip up the flooded tunnel when they had staggered out nearly frozen.

Larry lifted up one set of breathing apparatus and fitted the bottles between Linda's shoulder blades while she fastened the harness. When he had finished she helped him with his own and then they sat down to adjust their face plates and flippers. The face plate pulled painfully at Larry's split cheek when he fitted it on but he fought down the sharp exclamation of pain. Now was no time to worry about minor discomforts. He swopped his Luger for the spear-gun and checked that the underwater weapon was ready to fire. The now useless pistol he left in the pocket of his jacket.

He stood up and helped Linda to her feet and for a few moments they practised breathing through the mouthpieces attached to the oxygen bottles. The flow of air seemed regular enough and Larry decided that they would have to take a chance on the equipment working perfectly. There was no reason why it shouldn't.

Larry released the mouthpiece and said, 'Let's get going. I'll go first with this little toy' — he patted the spear-gun — 'you follow me with the torch. If you see any sign of Rogart or any of those big rats just flick the torch off once. That'll be the quickest way of warning me. In fact you'd better make it once for a rat and twice for Rogart — if there's time.' He put his free arm around her waist and when she nodded he led her down towards the black surface of the flooded tunnel.

It was difficult to walk in the ungainly flippers and they splashed rather clumsily into the water.

'Make it fast,' advised Larry. He was thinking that eventually the cold must penetrate through their thick rubber clothing.

They splashed swiftly through the shallower parts of the tunnel, feeling the black sea swirl up around their legs. Linda found herself thinking of the giant rat that had attacked them before, and she shuddered. The thick rubber of their suits would protect them from the rodent's teeth if there were any of the rats left to attack, but after Larry had fired his single spear they would have nothing but the knives in their belts to defend themselves. The thought made her shudder again and Larry's arm tightened about her as they waded further into the depths of the flooded galleries.

The water became waist deep and they passed the open tunnel mouth where the last rat had attacked. Here Larry stopped.

'We'll start swimming from here,' he told her. 'We'll get along faster that way and we don't want to be down here too long. Just keep behind me and we'll follow this tunnel to the main shaft.'

She glanced around the damp and rotting walls, trickling with water that dripped and splashed into the sea. Weird shadows were again dancing in the light of her torch and she had a sudden feeling that even the silent watery depths ahead couldn't be quite as chilling as this.

'All right,' she said. 'We'll swim as fast as we can and get it over.'

She pulled her face plate down and fitted the mouth-piece between her lips. Larry followed suit and saw her nod before plunging forward along the flooded gallery. The black sea swirled around his face plate as he swam into the gloom. He looked back and saw Linda swimming after him and then surged on. Even though he had to use one hand to carry his gun he still made swift progress, the large flippers driving him easily forward. Linda surged in his wake holding the torch ahead of her.

Fear of the eventual cold eating through to them made them swim much faster than they would have normally done through such dangerous waters. Already they were feeling chilled despite the rubber suits. They swam on beneath the slime-streaked walls and roof of the old mine. The atmosphere of death and decay was almost as cold as the black sea.

The horizon where the roof met the sea was soon reached and Larry ducked his head under and swam down. The claustrophobic feeling as the icy waters closed above his head made his stomach turn, but he kept on without hesitation. He thought instinctively of Linda but the light from the torch was still with him so she had to be all right. Even so he had to turn his head to make sure. He saw her as a dim shadow behind the white glare from the centre of her torch-beam.

She saw him glance back and put on a sudden spurt until she came level underneath him. The tunnel was too narrow for them to swim side by side but at least they could swim one above the other. The fast swishing of their legs and the big flippers drove them on through the flooded tunnel. The walls, in the light of the torch, where thick with dark green slime and weed. Short tentacles from the underwater jungle waved an eerie greeting in the disturbance of their passage. More, longer, fronds reached up from the uneven tunnel floor only to sway back as they passed overhead. Beyond the range of the torch lay only the utter blackness and silence of the grave.

Larry felt slightly more at ease now that Linda was below him where he could see her. The light from her torch was shining further ahead of him now that she was level and that too was a help. A stream of bubbles trailed behind them along the tunnel but neither of them looked back. They had eyes only for the way ahead. They came to a fork but Larry still had the memory of the map they had stolen clear in his mind. He led the way unhesitatingly to the right. He knew they had to be nearing the main shaft now. He wondered where Rogart was waiting.

They passed many branching tunnels that disappeared into the flooded maze, dark and gaping holes in the rotting walls where faint cross currents of motion brought fear leaping into their hearts. Nowhere was the slight pull of the sea strong enough to affect their course, but there was always the chilling thought that the next one might be. And if they were once sucked up one of those side tunnels and lost in the flooded galleries they would die; doomed to swim through the silent darkness until their air ran out and they lost consciousness in their sunken tomb.

During the first few seconds underwater the salt sea water had soaked through the bandages around Larry's blood-stained cheek and stung like the caress of a thousand nettles. Now, the cold was numbing the flesh and he could no longer feel it. The cold was beginning to penetrate everywhere and he wondered how long they would have before they were numbed into unconsciousness.

The tunnel began to widen suddenly, and he knew they must be getting near. His hand tightened around the spear-gun and he peered into the gloom beyond the beam of the torch. The fallen shaft had to be just ahead and at any time now they could encounter Rogart or the last of the rat pack. Linda began to gain height until she was swimming beside him. He gave her a tight-lipped smile, but in the gloom he could not distinguish her features behind her face plate so it was unlikely that she could distinguish his.

The tunnel opened out abruptly into a wide underwater cavern where half a dozen tunnels converged. In the dead centre was a high mound of fallen debris which rose like an undersea mountain to the roof. Larry knew that that mountain marked the foot of the main surface shaft. The shaft that had collapsed around him as he was pulled up. They moved in slowly and Larry took the torch from Linda's hand. They circled the fallen earth and rock until something white gleamed in the torchbeam. The something white was a human skull, its eyes the watery black of the sea. Beyond it gleamed the rib cage and then the rest was buried beneath the fall. The body must have been picked clean by the rats.

They both shivered.

Larry wondered which of his three companions the skeleton represented and couldn't get the thought out of his mind. They moved on.

There were no more bones, so it seemed that the other two had been completely buried when the shaft caved in. Around them their escaping air was tracing bubbly patterns through the black depths. Weed and slime covered everything. Larry had the spear-gun ready in one hand and the torch in the other as he propelled himself along with his feet. Linda kept as close to him as possible. Like giant, ungainly, fish they nosed around the sunken mound, and then they spotted the haversack.

They closed in on it like sharks on a dying swimmer. It lay clear of the fallen shaft, the old canvas smothered in slime. Larry turned it over by the old shoulder straps and saw that it had been unopened. So they had beaten Rogart to it. He tried to lift it but it was heavy. The clumsy bulk of it would delay them badly in getting back to the surface so he made up his mind to open it there and then. He used the butt of the spear-gun as a lever to snap open the straps. Carefully he pulled up the flap.

Linda watched as he reached inside. He fumbled for a moment with one hand, then gave her the torch. Tipping up the haversack he pulled it away from the contents. A large box slid slowly on to the seabed. It was like a medium sized suitcase and it took only a couple of minutes to insert the knife from his belt into the clasps and break them. Slowly

Larry lifted the lid.

The box contained a radio set, a rusted two way transmitter complete with microphone and head phones. It was totally ruined by the sea. For a moment Larry stared at it and then he noticed something else, a small flat packet, wrapped in oilskin, tucked down the side of the radio. He pulled it out and in the same moment Linda touched his shoulder urgently.

He looked up and saw that her eyes were wide and afraid behind her mask. She raised one arm and pointed meaningly.

His gaze followed the direction of her pointing finger. Still far away a light was moving towards them down one of the flooded tunnels. A light that moved swiftly through the watery blackness of the old mine.

It could only be Rogart.

21

Duel in the Darkness

Larry watched as the wavering torchlight came closer. As yet he could see nothing of the frogman behind it. Rogart was coming down a different tunnel from the one they had followed and it was clear what must have happened. Rogart must have taken the wrong turning back at the fork and become lost in the maze of flooded galleries. Since then he had kept on swimming hopelessly through the old mine until he had spotted their light. Now he was closing in for the kill.

Larry gripped Linda's arm and made her look round at him. He indicated by pointing his finger that she was to remain in that one spot. She nodded slowly, a grotesque figure framed by escaping air bubbles. He turned away with his heart pounding and swam to meet Rogart.

He could dimly make out the figure

of the other frogman now, and saw the spear-gun at the ready in the other's hand. He raised his own grimly, all along he had known it would have to end like this, with these weapons, but now it seemed suddenly unreal. It was like swimming through a dream, only it was a dream he had to see through — there was no waking up.

He was holding the flat packet he had taken from the haversack in the same hand as his torch. He transferred it to his gun hand and held it up in the light. He wanted to make sure of drawing Rogart's attack to himself, and he knew that packet had to be the mysterious something that the other wanted. Rogart slackened his pace and began to circle through the black depths as Larry tucked the packet safely into his belt.

They hovered in the silent darkness. Each had only one spear — one chance. Each knew that only one of them could swim away alive.

Alone in the inky blackness Linda could only pray. Pray that her presence would give Larry that extra incentive to win.

And Larry was thinking exactly what she knew he would think. Linda was with him and he had to win. For her sake he couldn't afford to lose.

They circled warily through the black depths of the mine. Each striving to break the other's nerve. The cold, nerve tearing, silence hemmed them in. There was absolutely no sound. Nothing stirred in the black waters except themselves. The weed fronds that grew from the rotten timbers that shored up the walls waved slow taunting tendrils every time they were caught in the wavering torchlight. The tension grew to screaming pitch. Someone *had* to break.

Rogart erupted into a flurry of movement. He surged forwards and then flipped upwards and away like a wriggling torpedo. Larry kicked himself desperately to one side, forcing himself to hold his fire. Rogart's black-suited form shot away and then turned cautiously back. Larry gritted his teeth, that manœuvre had been deliberately calculated to draw his fire; to fluster him into hastily launching his only spear. Leaving Rogart a clear run in for the kill.

They circled again and then Larry saw a faint figure swimming out of the blackness to Rogart's left. It was Linda. The sight made his stomach tremble with fear but there was nothing he could do but watch. Rogart sensed her and wheeled in the sea. His gun came up as she kicked away but he didn't fire at her weaving form. He spun back quickly, moving sideways as he covered Larry's approach. Larry knew then that he didn't have to fear for Linda. Rogart had to kill him first and he had only one spear. While he lived Linda was safe.

Rogart came in again, his spear-gun swinging slowly against the pressure of the water. Again Larry took avoiding action rather than loose his only spear. Rogart dived low, his chest scraping the tunnel floor as he turned aside.

Larry surged in, playing Rogart's own game — a feint attack and a weaving breakaway that just might draw a hasty shot. Rogart rolled over on to his back and flipped himself away. Larry turned aside, rolling desperately to avoid an unexpected shot that never came. Rogart was still afraid to fire until he was absolutely sure of a hit.

They circled again, fighting a weird duel of nerves in the black depths. Neither dared get too close to the other, each strove to panic his opponent into a hasty shot. Twice Linda moved in silently in an effort to attract Rogart's attention but except for wary glances he ignored her. She had no gun and dared not swim too close to the combatants. She knew that if Rogart could manœuvre her between them he could move in and kill. If she were in the way Larry would not fire and Rogart could use her as a shield. She had to stay out of range.

Twice more Rogart attempted to draw Larry's single spear with abrupt flustering movements. He failed each time. The air bubbles around them were now thick under the rotting roof and every weed was waving angrily from the disturbance they had created in the silent sea. The cracks in the rotten timbers seemed to leer at them like grinning mouths. Every knothole was a weirdly gleaming eye. The proximity of death grew clearer as the tension mounted.

Someone *had* to break.

They had backed apart when Rogart suddenly flattened out and surged forward. He nosed in with deadly speed, making the smallest possible target. Larry rolled, spiralling through the flooded depths, he knew instinctively that this was it. Rogart turned to follow him and dropped his torch. He used both hands to force his spear-gun round as Larry twisted away. He squeezed the trigger and swerved aside.

Larry heard the hiss of air as the vicious barbed spear zipped past his shoulder. He brought his own gun up and saw Rogart's black shape swerving away. He followed the turning figure with his torch and then fired. A second hiss of air sounded as the spear whipped forward. It buried itself deep into Rogart's stomach and carried the man back.

Larry dropped his empty spear-gun and kicked his way over to his dying enemy. Linda swam down out of the blackness and picked up the man's fallen torch. They converged together upon the limp frogman and Larry supported the man and peered close at his face. Rogart still had his lips clamped about the mouthpiece of the oxygen tube and appeared to be still breathing. Larry glanced at the ugly steel spear that jutted from the man's body and realized that Rogart was as good as dead but even so he couldn't leave him. The idea of deserting even Rogart to the rats was repulsive. He got one hand under the man's armpit and started to tow him back along the tunnel down which they had come. The flat package was still in his belt so there was nothing to delay them in the mine. Linda followed him closely.

They swam as fast as they could through the flooded galleries, practically racing back with lusty movements of their legs. They followed the same direct tunnel and it was only a matter of minutes before they broke surface to find the roof only a foot or so above their heads. They kept going until they reached chest-deep water and here Larry stopped to remove Rogart's face plate and breathing tube so that he could breathe normally.

The man's lips were pasty but his eyes were open. He looked at them with no expression. He might have been a dead fish.

Linda said quietly, 'He's going, Larry, we'll never get him out of the mine.'

Larry was holding the man upright and knew that what Linda had said was true. He had never expected Rogart to last this long with that spear in him. But there were still questions he wanted to ask. He said quietly:

'Can you tell us about it, Rogart, it can't matter to you now?'

Rogart's lips moved. 'Swine,' he got out weakly, 'if — if only you hadn't come along.'

'Who was Konrad?' Larry persisted gently.

'Konrad — Hans Konrad, he was a Nazi agent who was sent here in World War II. A fishing boat landed him on the coast near here.' Rogart paused and choked a little, he stirred in Larry's arms. He seemed too far gone to feel any pain.

He went on weakly: 'Konrad had bad luck. He broke — broke a leg. It was dawn so he had to hide. He hid in this mine. God — God only knows how he got up and down but he did. He was — was a tough devil.'

He choked again and they had to wait for him to recover a bit more of his failing strength.

'Konrad made it to my house.' The words were lower. 'I was in German pay. I was his contact. I radioed a ship to take him back. Later he — he died on another mission. I — I didn't know he'd left the haversack in the mine until this year.'

He moved again in Larry's arms his lips were bloodless now.

Larry asked softly, 'How did you find out, about the pack?'

Rogart rallied a little. 'Konrad's sister . . . a girl called Greta. She came to England for . . . a holiday. She looked me up. Hans had told her all about me . . . about his missions. She — she scared me when I knew who she was. She talked about Konrad . . . wanted to thank me. Then she told me about the book — '

He subsided and hung limp in Larry's arms. For a moment they thought he was dead. Then his lips moved soundlessly, he moved weakly, very weakly, as though trying to get more comfortable.

Larry said softly, 'What about the book, Rogart?'

'Book — book of names. Names of his contacts. Konrad was very . . . worried about it. If the Nazis . . . Nazis knew he had them on paper he could have been — have been shot. So he told the girl . . . he told her everything. She told me . . . she thought that with the war over nothing mattered any more.'

'Why did it matter?' Larry couldn't keep the slight trace of urgency out of his tone.

The bloodless mouth twisted into a smile, humour came back momentarily to the cold green eyes. 'Isn't it obvious, Mr. Brown. My name was in that book.

It could — could hang me for treason. There were also nine other names. Nine perfect set-ups for blackmail. I could have made those others pay — pay well . . . if not them . . . their families. I could have become rich — '

He wrenched suddenly out of Larry's grasp as he spoke, summoning the last of his fading strength in one final effort. The move took Larry completely by surprise and he realized that Rogart had talked for one reason only. While they talked Rogart had been stealthily sliding a gun out of his belt. It was wound in oilcloth and Larry could see the muffled shape of it in Rogart's rising hand.

Rogart was reeling backwards in the black sea. His green eyes gleamed in the torchlight as he aimed the shrouded gun. Larry flung himself forward desperately as Rogart fumbled to get his finger on the trigger through the thick oilcloth. Those wrappings hampered Rogart and saved Larry's life. He closed with the dying killer and forced the weak gun hand back. Rogart had no strength to resist but still he found the trigger and pulled. The gun roared and the bullet whined up the tunnel to smack into the roof twenty yards behind them.

The roar of sound and the impact of the bullet vibrated through the narrow crumbling tunnel, and then like a roar of thunder the whole roof came crashing down. Tons of rock and earth tumbled into the sea just beyond them and forced the black water back up the tunnel like a tidal wave. The force of it rose above them and swept all three off their feet. They went under, choking in the swirling black water, their ears filled with the rumble of the collapsing tunnel. Stark fear filled Larry as he let go of Rogart. Another body collided into him and he grabbed it thankfully. At least he still held Linda.

The water swirled and steadied and the thunder died to sporadic splashings as they fought their way upright. The sudden fall of the tunnel roof had forced the water level up by a good twelve inches. The whole tunnel was now completely blocked. Larry held Linda up as she spluttered and spat and then heard a rasping chuckle from behind. Their two torches were floating on the agitated surface and casting crazed flickerings around the surface of the sea. They saw Rogart hanging against the rotten shoring, his eyes wild and blood smearing his mouth.

'You're trapped, you swine. Trapped like a rat in a bloody trap!'

He almost shouted the words, flinging into them the last of his strength. The laugh that followed was drowned as he slid beneath the surface and died.

22

No Turning Back

Larry stared bitterly at the spot where Rogart had disappeared. Linda was clinging to him and he put his arms around her hopelessly. The swirling water was almost steady now and washing around their chins. Occasionally lumps of earth or stone still bounced down the slope of the roof fall and splashed into the sea. They were trapped, twenty yards in one direction the surface of the sea joined with the tunnel roof, fifteen yards towards their rear the fall blocked their path. He felt the cold eating into his stomach, and the girl quivering against him.

Silence reigned in the mine. The floating torches were steadier now but still traced weird shadows among the fungous slime that covered the walls. Rogart had not come up and the weight of his diving kit must have held him down to the tunnel floor. The claustrophobic atmosphere became almost unbearable.

Linda said shakily: 'What now, Larry?' Her tone was faltering and her face white in the gloom.

Larry reached out to pick up one of the torches. He shone it around their grim prison slowly. He didn't know how to answer her question. How could he answer it? What could they do?

He thought hopefully of the police and the dog teams who had been closing in on them before they descended the mine. It was a forlorn hope. Even if the police were right behind them and had heard the shot they would be too late. By the time they broke through the barrier of earth and rubble he and Linda would be dead. Already the bitter cold of the underground sea was eating into them. Even if their air lasted they would freeze before any rescuer reached them.

Linda said: 'Everything was so nearly over. It just doesn't seem fair that he should win after all.' She was almost in tears.

He held her tighter. 'We'll get out — somehow.'

His words were confident, reassuring, now all he needed was for someone to reassure him. He told himself desperately that there must be a way out. After all this he just couldn't let Linda drown.

He waved his torch and the black sea gleamed at him maliciously. A trickle of water ran through the slime on the walls. The cold ate into his stomach.

Linda said angrily: 'All we had to do was get the police to trace that Konrad girl. They could have found her easy enough and she could have verified everything about that haversack. The police would have had no reason to doubt us then. With her and that book you've got you could have been cleared. No one would disbelieve your story about Crane.'

'Easy, Linda.' He spoke soothingly, glad that anger had replaced her near crying. 'All we've got to do now is get out.'

She never answered but he felt her press tighter against him. Already he was beginning to feel smothered by the air of decay. He stared around him frantically, seeking for some way out. And then as he stared at the surface of the sea the answer came. The sea had broken in — and where the sea broke in there had to be a way out.

He remembered the map and the one long tunnel that had stretched out under the sea bed. Somewhere along that tunnel there had to be an opening where the sea rushed in. An opening that would let them out into the sea itself. It was worth a try. It was their only chance.

He said eagerly: 'Linda, we're leaving. We're going out where the sea comes in. There's only one tunnel that leads out beneath the sea bed and that leads out direct from here. We can escape into the sea and swim ashore.'

She looked at him slowly — and then she smiled.

'Of course, if the sea can come in, we can go out.' She laughed suddenly. 'We'll beat him yet, Larry. We'll beat him yet.'

'Come on then.' He refitted his mask

over his face. 'Let's get out of here before it gets too cold. Grab that other torch and keep with me, I'm pretty sure I can remember the way from the map.'

He watched her pull her mask over her face and then fit the breathing tube into her mouth. He fitted his own while she retrieved the second torch and then nodded. Together they dived and swam back into the depths of the flooded mine.

As she drew level beneath him Larry thought again of his self-adopted motto when he had bluffed his way north. It was still a good game to win.

They swam fast to fight off the increasing cold on the way back towards the fallen shaft where they had found the haversack. With two torches the way was not so gloomy but the sea behind them was as black as ever. Larry realized grimly that they would have to find the exit to the sea-bed the first time for they would have no other chance. Their air might last but the cold would kill them. Already it was like swimming through black liquid ice.

There would be no turning back.

They reached the wide underwater cavern where the main tunnels converged at the fallen shaft. The recent duelling ground was still and silent and they swam across and around the mountain of rubble that marked the shaft. Larry hesitated a little on the far side and checked that he was directly opposite the tunnel mouth they had left before leading Linda on. He could only pray now that his memory of the map had been good and that this was the correct tunnel. If this was not the gallery that had let in the sea then they would drown, as Rogart had said, like rats in a trap.

The way here was thickly congested with weed and slime and it was clear that this particular tunnel had been submerged for much longer than the higher ones behind them. It was a promising sign and they swam on all the faster, nosing through the rotting tunnels amid a swirl of trapped bubbles.

The gallery seemed to stretch for miles and all the way Larry was haunted by the terrible conviction that he had taken the wrong turning. The thought that they were swimming deeper and deeper into a dead end hundreds of feet below the earth made his head ache and his stomach squirm. He kept thinking of Linda swimming strongly below him, thinking and praying.

She glanced up at him many times, trusting in his leadership. The cold was numbing her now and it was mostly willpower that propelled her along. There was nothing she could do now except trust him and hope, and swim on into the close underwater world.

The weeds that clogged the tunnel floor grew higher, weaving and bending at their approach. It forced Linda to swim upwards for she was afraid of getting caught. Several times as she kicked back her legs knocked into Larry's. He climbed to give her more room until his oxygen bottles were bumping on the tunnel roof. Strange splintered arms from broken boards reached out at them as they passed. Several times Larry had to push them aside. He was almost numb now and he knew Linda could not be much better.

Abruptly the tunnel ended. It ended in a steep upward slope that brought dread to both their hearts. The tunnel was a dead end gallery. And they were trapped. They swam on more slowly and then abruptly new hoped flared. Where the roof and the sloping level of the tunnel floor joined there was a blacker patch. A patch where the old boards that shored up the roof ended in splintered edges. Larry swam up to it and shone his torch upwards. Up through a large hole that could only lead up to the sea bed.

He half turned with a flick of his flippers and brought himself almost face to face with Linda. He pointed to the hole in the roof and saw her lips form the semblance of a smile behind her mask. He gave her arm a firm squeeze and then kicked upwards through the hole. The hole widened as he swam up until he came out of a large pit and realized that he was in the open sea. Linda swam up beside him and hand in hand they struck out for the surface.

The sea was fairly calm as their heads broke the surface and they bobbed together like sluggish corks in a bath. A hundred yards away the waves were breaking on the moonlit coastline and they swam strongly towards it. They jettisoned the face masks and oxygen bottles as they swam and finally staggered wearily up a small sandy beach among the rocks.

Perhaps it was the same beach where the Nazi agent Hans Konrad had landed all those years before. They neither knew nor cared. They fell on the sand and Linda rolled against Larry, crushing against her shivering body.

'Warm me, Larry,' she begged. 'Warm me.' She hugged him tightly as his lips found hers. Her lips were cold and tasted of salt but he hardly noticed. He kissed her fervently and sought to instil warmth into her numb limbs by burying her in the sand with the weight of his own body. He felt the wild beating of her heart, and then miraculously the blood began to flow through her veins. Her mouth became warm and alive again. Moist and vibrant under his own.

After a long time he raised his

shrouded face with its angry red stain and looked down at her. 'Well,' he said quietly. 'Shall we give ourselves up?'

She smiled. 'That's all we have to do now, isn't it. Once the police trace the Konrad girl she'll be able to confirm enough of your story to convince them that it's true. She'll be able to tell them about her brother and the haversack. and prove that Rogart was in German pay during the war. Once the police know why Crane needed that haversack they'll have to believe it was his gun you used. And a word with that colonel who originally owned those giant rats should convince them that you had good reason to fire it as an act of mercy. They can't disbelieve you now that we can give them the full story.'

'You're right, provided we can get the Konrad girl to come forward.' Larry was still slightly doubtful.

'She'll come, she's got nothing to hide. Besides, she must have been issued with a passport to get here, so the police will be able to trace her through the German passport office. We've got nothing to worry about.'

Larry grinned and kissed her lightly on the nose. 'All right, you've convinced me. But first I want to see what all the trouble was about. Before we give ourselves up I'm going to have a look at that book.' He pulled the bound package he had taken from Konrad's pack out of his belt, and she watched with interest as he unwound the oilskin covering. He unveiled a large leather wallet and carefully tipped the contents onto the sand between them. There were ration cards, and clothing cards, together with other papers that were unrecognizable. Among them was a small black pocket book. Larry opened it and leafed through the damp pages, separating them with difficulty.

Linda's cheek was touching his own bandaged one when the ironic truth slowly dawned. For a moment their faces were blank, and then Linda chuckled softly. Larry laughed with her and they almost collapsed back on the sand. After all they had been through it left them almost hysterical.

They almost wished that Rogart were alive then. It was the kind of bitter joke that would have appealed to his callous sense of humour — had it been directed to someone else.

During the sixteen years that the book had been lost in the mine the sea water had penetrated into the protecting oilskin covering. The names in the little black book that could have made Rogart a fortune in blackmail, or convicted him of high treason, had the evidence fallen into police hands, were all totally illegible.

The gentle irony of it could not be bettered.

THE END

MURDER AS USUAL
Hugh Pentecost
A psychotic girl shot and killed Mac Crenshaw, who had come to the New England town with the advance party for Senator Farraday. Private detective David Cotter agreed that the girl was probably just a pawn in a complex game — but who had sent her on the assignment?

THE MARGIN
Ian Stuart
It is rumoured that Walkers Brewery has been selling arms to the South African army, and Graham Lorimer is asked to investigate. He meets the beautiful Shelley van Rynveld, who is dedicated to ending apartheid. When a Walkers employee is killed in a hit-and-run accident, his wife tells Graham that he's been seeing Shelly van Rynveld . . .

TOO LATE FOR THE FUNERAL
Roger Ormerod

Carol Turner, seventeen, and a mystery, is very close to a murder, and she has in her possession a weapon that could prove a number of things. But it is Elsa Mallin who suffers most before the truth of Carol Turner releases her.

NIGHT OF THE FAIR
Jay Baker

The gun was the last of the things for which Harry Judd had fought and now it was in the hands of his worst enemy, aimed at the boy he had tried to help. This was the night in which the past had to be faced again and finally understood.

MR CRUMBLESTONE'S EDEN

Henry Crumblestone was a quiet little man who would never knowingly have harmed another, and it was a dreadful twist of irony that caused him to kill in defence of a dream . . .

PAY-OFF IN SWITZERLAND
Bill Knox

'Hot' British currency was being smuggled to Switzerland to be laundered, hidden in a safari-style convoy heading across Europe. Jonathan Gaunt, external auditor for the Queen's and Lord Treasurer's Remembrancer, went along with the safari, posing as a tourist, to get any lead he could. But sudden death trailed the convoy every kilometer to Lake Geneva.

SALVAGE JOB
Bill Knox

A storm has left the oil tanker S.S. *Craig Michael* stranded and almost blocking the only channel to the bay at Cabo Esco. Sent to investigate, marine insurance inspector Laird discovers that the Portuguese bay is hiding a powder keg of international proportions.

BOMB SCARE — FLIGHT 147
Peter Chambers

Smog delayed Flight 147, and so prevented a bomb exploding in mid-air. Walter Keane found that during the crisis he had been robbed of his jewel bag, and Mark Preston was hired to locate it without involving the police. When a murder was committed, Preston knew the stake had grown.

STAMBOUL INTRIGUE
Robert Charles

Greece and Turkey were on the brink of war, and the conflict could spell the beginning of the end for the Western defence pact of N.A.T.O. When the rumour of a plot to speed this possibility reached Counter-espionage in Whitehall, Simon Larren and Adrian Cleyton were despatched to Turkey . . .

CRACK IN THE SIDEWALK
Basil Copper

After brilliant scientist Professor Hopcroft is knocked down and killed by a car, L.A. private investigator Mike Faraday discovers that his death was murder and that differing groups are engaged in a power struggle for The Zetland Method. As Mike tries to discover what The Zetland Method is, corpses and hair-breadth escapes come thick and fast . . .

DEATH OF A MACHINE
Charles Leader

When Mike M'Call found the mutilated corpse of a marine in an alleyway in Singapore, a thousand-strong marine battalion was hell-bent on revenge for their murdered comrade — and the next target for the tong gang of paid killers appeared to be M'Call himself . . .

ANYONE CAN MURDER
Freda Bream
Hubert Carson, the editorial Manager of the Herald Newspaper in Auckland, is found dead in his office. Carson's fellow employees knew that the unpopular chief reporter, Clive Yarwood, wanted Carson's job — but did he want it badly enough to kill for it?

CART BEFORE THE HEARSE
Roger Ormerod
Sometimes a case comes up backwards. When Ernest Connelly said 'I have killed . . . ', he did not name the victim. So Dave Mallin and George Coe find themselves attempting to discover a body to fit the crime.

SALESMAN OF DEATH
Charles Leader
For Mike M'Call, selling guns in Detroit proves a dangerous business — from the moment of his arrival in the middle of a racial plot, to the final clash of arms between two rival groups of militant extremists.

THE FOURTH SHADOW
Robert Charles

Simon Larren merely had to ensure that the visiting President of Maraquilla remained alive during a goodwill tour of the British Crown Colony of San Quito. But there were complications. Finally, there was a Communist-inspired bid for illegal independence from British rule, backed by the evil of voodoo.

SCAVENGERS AT WAR
Charles Leader

Colonel Piet Van Velsen needed an experienced officer for his mercenary commando, and Mike M'Call became a reluctant soldier. The Latin American Republic was torn apart by revolutionary guerrilla groups — but why were the ruthless Congo veterans unleashed on a province where no guerrilla threat existed?

MENACES, MENACES
Michael Underwood

Herbert Sipson, professional black-mailer, was charged with demanding money from a bingo company. Then, a demand from the Swallow Sugar Corporation also bore all the hallmarks of a Sipson scheme. But it arrived on the opening day of Herbert's Old Bailey trial — so how could he have been responsible?

MURDER WITH MALICE
Nicholas Blake

At the Wonderland holiday camp, someone calling himself The Mad Hatter is carrying out strange practical jokes that are turning increasingly malicious. Private Investigator Nigel Strangeways follows the Mad Hatter's trail and finally manages to make sense of the mayhem.

THE LONG NIGHT
Hartley Howard

Glenn Bowman is awakened by the 'phone ringing in the early hours of the morning and a woman he does not know invites him over to her apartment. When she tells him she wishes she was dead, he decides he ought to go and talk to her. It is a decision he is to bitterly regret when he finds himself involved in a case of murder . . .

THE LONELY PLACE
Basil Copper

The laconic L.A. private investigator Mike Faraday is hired to discover who is behind the death-threats to millionaire ex-silent movie star Francis Bolivar. Faraday finds a strange state of affairs at Bolivar's Gothic mansion, leading to a horrifying mass slaughter when a chauffeur goes berserk.

THE DARK MIRROR
Basil Copper
Californian private eye Mike Faraday reckons the case is routine, until a silenced gun cuts down Horvis the antique dealer and involves Mike in a trail of violence and murder.

DEADLY NIGHTCAP
Harry Carmichael
Mrs. Esther Payne was a very unpopular lady — right up to the night when she took two sleeping tablets and died. Traces of strychnine were discovered in the tube of pills, but only four people had the opportunity to obtain the poison for Esther's deadly night-cap . . .

DARK DESIGN
Freda Hurt
Caroline Lane missed her husband when he was away on his frequent business trips — until the mysterious phone-call that introduced Neil Fuller into her life. Then came doubts that led her to question her husband's real whereabouts, even his identity.

ESCAPE A KILLER
Judson Philips

Blinded by an acid-throwing fanatic, famous newspaperman Max Richmond moved to an isolated mansion in Connecticut. On a visit there, Peter Styles, a writer for NEWSVIEW MAGAZINE, became involved in a diabolical plot. The trap was not meant for him, but he was as helpless as the intended victim.

LONG RANGE DESERTER
David Bingley

Jack Walmer deserts from the French Foreign Legion to fight with a British Unit. Time and again, Jack must prove his allegiance by risking his life to save British servicemen. His final task is an attack on an Italian fortress, where the identity of a British prisoner holds the key to his future happiness.

THE FATAL TRIP
Michael Underwood

When Stephen Burley is convicted for theft from his employers, Detective Sergeant Nick Attwell, the investigating officer, is uneasy about the case. He appeals to his young wife, Clare, for help and, under various pretences, she embarks on some very tricky enquiries of her own . . .

THE SUN VIRGIN
Robert Charles

A search for Inca gold was the challenge held out to Peter Conway by his brother Steve. What Steve forgot to mention was that the man whom Peter was to replace on the expedition had already been murdered — and there was more than one interested party ready to lie, steal and even kill for the Inca fortune.

CUSTOMER SERVICE EXCELLENCE

Libraries & Archives

Kent
County
Council